The Avenue Journal

Issue VIII - Anticipation

EDITORIAL STAFF

Chris Kosmides - Editor in Chief
is an editor and writer who currently lives in Baltimore.

Jonathan Tomick - Senior Editor
is a writer, editor and educator, currently residing in Baltimore.

Pamela McGinnis- Associate Editor
is a writer and editor who lives in Baltimore.

Tera Smith - Graphic Artist
is a Baltimore-based designer.

Table of Contents

The Wrestle with Ready
Torrey Francis Malek

I am, at this very moment, in a mighty wrestle with readiness.
I can feel it grasping and clawing at the meat over my wings.
I am unhinging, denaturing, unclasping like ancient door latches,
and if I am not cautious, my fingers will fall right out of their
caskets.

I can feel the ready rising,
outgrowing the size of me,
and all I can do is sit here,
all I can do is be here and be
ready.

Well, I'm ready.
On the cusp of something.
On the brink of something.
On the edge of a ledge of, something.
On like a light switch looking up at the sky,
on like an eyelid prying open for dawn,
all aflame because I decided it was time
to look up.
To look on.

So now, I'm ready.
Though not at all in agreement that I am.
My guts are in a clamour.
My lungs are funnelling gusts.
My feet are playing a rudderless drum set.
My head is heating up a baked brain
bound down by a wool bonnet.
Yet I know that I'm ready.
Even if we may not all agree. I am.

Ready.
I'm pinning down ready,
razing down ready,
at any moment, shaky,
stern, and steady, at the ready,
and when my legs push,
I'll shoot past plaster of sky
toward the highs I set my sights on.
because I know that I'll reach them.

Because I know-

Because I know.

Predawn Attack
Linda Marshall

Waking up slowly, Kate does a quick scan of the bedroom without moving a muscle, her eyes darting from side to side. Was that him she heard moving around, or something else? The air conditioner? The fan? Something outside? He likes to patrol the house early in the morning, looking for signs of life. He's a skulker, so it's important she remain absolutely still.

Careful not to make the slightest noise, she gradually lifts her right arm out from under the sheets, moving her hand to the dresser next to the bed, her fingers blindly and silently searching the surface for her glasses. Did he hear her? No? Good. Then, like the game of pick-up-sticks she used to play as a child at her grandparents' home, she gingerly picks up her folded glasses from the dresser without disturbing anything else, finding them as though reading Braille.

Lifting them gingerly, avoiding brushing her hand against anything else on the dresser — alarm clock, phone, and knickknacks filling every inch — she brings the reading glasses in slow motion towards her welcoming eyes.

Her bladder is full, but getting out of bed to go into the bathroom is out of the question. He'd spot her immediately and make his demands known, so she endures. All she wants is a few more minutes of solitude, undetected. That's all.

The next task, using her right arm again, is to retrieve her book from the same dresser, the book strategically propped up in a partially-open drawer. If the drawer creaks, or the bed springs squeak as she leans toward the dresser, or something inside the drawer is jostled in the process, it's all over. He'll know. With his keen sense of sight and hearing, he'll know. She feels like a prisoner in her own home. Every day it's the same thing, over and over again, with the same outcome…the Myth of Sisyphus.

Carefully, so carefully, she lifts the book out of the drawer, then slides it over her nightgown like a low-flying plane avoiding radar detection till it's right next to her face, all the while avoiding glances in his direction. If at any point she inadvertently makes eye contact with him, it's over. But out of the corner of her eye, she thinks she can see him, partially concealed, still asleep across the room. She turns one page of her book, then the next and the next, silently reading, a statue in repose.

But, no. The bending of the paper as she turns the page, or her breathing — now a beat or two higher — or the mere shifting of molecules in the air — who knows? — alerts his sense of vigilance, and in a flash he's standing right next to the bed, inches from her, staring holes through her. *I will not be tricked*, he seems to be telling her with his eyes, with his body language.

"Oh, all right," she relents, sighing, sitting up and swinging her legs off the side of the bed, tossing her book aside. "All I wanted was five more minutes. That's all. Five minutes. Was that too much to ask? Why can't you wait?"

He says nothing, of course, but his dark brown eyes soften at the sight of her getting out of bed. He looks at her with such love that she leans down, pets the top of his furry brown head and kisses his soft muzzle. Together they make their way downstairs in the day's early light to the darkened kitchen, where she will prepare his breakfast and then take him for a walk.....There's always tomorrow.

The Last Mile
Valerie Wong

how to guard this great
buoyant secret
swelling within my belly
threatening to burst
with every word i speak?
i've been silent for so long
it seems inhumane to swallow
bliss so engulfing
it feels like a shield
still i must contain myself
a little longer
fate is so easily tempted
and joy subject
to the threat of eclipse
i cannot risk having
this rug pulled out
from under me
so i curl back into
my billowing self
waiting for the tentative
to become absolute

- the last mile

Espial
Elizabeth Mason

When the hearing-impaired visit the amusement park,
the line for the ride that spins stretches to Hannah Barbara Land,
and the bustle of fifty thousand people is split by silence
and by half. Today we make alterations in the system of selling
pictures and the younger employees will have to go through training
again, except for Cheryl who wears the words, I sign, under
her name. The usual pounding holler of riders is replaced
by the incessant roar of the roller coaster, the hiss of breaks,
wince of coming to a complete stop. We forget the way that words
feel in our mouths; our tongues examine the gloss of incisors,
the palate's curve and hollow. We learn how to feel words
in the pulse of our wrists and the tightening of our fingers, the heavy
fatigue of muscles in our right hands. We must pay close attention
to their exit, waving with awkward gestures, performing ballet
combinations as a gymnast must perform between tricks on the balance
beam. We've left the microphone on the middle shelf of the cabinet
rubbing up against computer wires, electrical tape, and we wait
on each customer one at a time, let them tap us on the shoulder,
and point to what they want. We have to watch them laugh,
their mouths dropped and hanging open, without sound.

52 Stitches of a Teenage Mother
Frankie Soto

keep that inhale secure until her heart panics. Until lungs burn with a crippling
need for air. when blurriness is accompanied by that moment of numbness
she will know this is really happening.

five foot seven
barely two months into what seventeen brings–there was nothing sweet about sixteen with swollen feet & no party to be celebrated.

new woman structure stretching like medieval torture – marks can't be hidden
as easily as scars. laugh lines have not yet loved a wrinkle or kiss her smile the way
a teenager should.

This is the metamorphosis of flesh to rubber band. 52 stitches inching closer.
knee caps soft like morning avena. Doctors chanting to finish.

To the days of tying pampers with teeth. One hand pressing the microwave
to heat bottles, other hand Jordan buzzer beating diapers into the trash.
foot stirs rice and beans with free hand rocking me to sleep.

Push- to the woman you became even when praise was silent. The days we
walked upstairs of the Bronx projects with the addicts using the hallways as lairs.
Your grip is a promise that you have been through worse and never let go.

Papa hold my hand & just keep walking.

8

The Promise
Alice Friman

They opened her up
stem to stern—
mucked around, snipped
snapped and sent her home
with a baggie. Permanent.
Miserable. Two weeks later
and 988 miles away, her friend
collapsed on the sidewalk.
A stopped heart—code blue
and blotto—just short of
the proverbial white light
programmed to switch on
to see her out. Unzipped,
zapped and zipped up again
then sent home with a new
timer and a monitor with
a green eye to watch
over her sleep. Friends
joined at the hip across
the ether: e-mails and phone.
Sidekicks, 988 miles apart,
held together by poetry—
the exchange of it, the love.

That's one tale not written up
in *The Chronicle* or *Poetry*
or *APR*, all of which featurethe flashy, the new. Their story
is old, old as the green light
they kept lit for each other,
the traffic light that doesn't flash
but holds steady, that says
Go, that says *Write*. The light
that means I'm with you, that
means I'm here and watching.

Adjacence
Theadora Siranian

August 2020, after René Magritte's "The Lovers II" (1928)

My primary object is you
love, or, the image hovering
in my mind's eye, behind
closed lids, white veils, masks,
locked doors—something
small and animal about the need
for touch in order to claim
proximity to our own lives: I was
here, I existed. And now this
famishing for nearness, our senses
held day after day in thrall by
the open sky outside, the repeating,
returning crepuscule—or dawn,
who can say? Oh, to be loved
in this world, to be loved, to be.

First Date at Prohibition Bar
Terri Drake

The night wide open
hope is what we had
after the afternoon sun beat down
the curtains closed against oppressive heat
we were familiar strangers
lingering longer than we should
over cocktails and slurred words
we could have said we loved each other
we could have kissed and meant it

we could have kissed and meant it
we could have said we loved each other
over cocktails and slurred words
lingering longer than we should
we were familiar strangers
the curtains closed against oppressive heat
after the afternoon sun beat down
hope is what we had
the night wide open

Sauterelle
Dana Miller

Chapter 1: Selva Oscura (the first 10 paces of a divorce)

Like a cold-stunned turtle, both revived and brutalized by a rectal thermometer, Cymbie woke up on the incandescent beach of something like Half Moon Cay with the foam at her toes and the blood of her childhood pony encrusted on her pearline hands. Hands--she groggily thought. Empty containers people attached way too much meaning to. These particular chapped items of her own had played John Lennon's white piano. They had affixed the uninspired band stickers of her first boyfriend's half-defunct attempts at music to her naked, teenage body as an anniversary surprise and then peeled them off in the shower herself the next morning, with flailing anger and defeated bits of skin, after he failed to come home yet again that night. Hands did things like meet presidents and birth babies. They soothed circus lions and allowed blind people to "see." They collected and organized things of every nature. Things like shells. Girls like her. They recorded and erased whole histories. But...

Of any era there must be an end if it is to be defined. As with any death, the last few days of my marriage did nothing to prepare me for its automatic and permanent demise. I loved my husband. I love him still. But to successfully leave him I must focus on his weak points and not the lovely, glimmering shadow of what was once a great, though one-sided, love. I must drink the noxious nightshade potion (true vision) that would reverse the spell. I don't think they make antidotes for the kind of venom someone who is no longer complicit in your fairytale of them--because it is no longer serving their own selfish interests--can loose on a heart that knew no better. The pain is intense and fructified. Every moment it reinvents itself as a new specter of a former smile. I remember the shiny mornings of chemical poetry—I wonder if the drugs didn't do it—would we still part company? Will I ever indulge my hope again? For it feels like all feeling is hereby drowned. And with the same brash cruelty of a kitten in a bag. All the sweet moments of you and my family. Every flower, all the moons, a million parts to asymmetry. Our long history of pain and renewal stopped when I began. I remember I saw you, pitied you last. And I remember foreign sand.

The rapidity of my family's sloughing off of my marital facades both frightened and edified me. I am the most hateful of bitches. I saw his tatty suitcase half-packed and was glad it was leaving. But when he kicked it in regretful giving up/admittance one night when he was leaving, I cried for hours and knew it would be an image to haunt me for all time--also that these would be the last tears of my truest girlhood heart. The rest of me would cry differently from there forward. I saw his toolbox sitting dusty on a slanted shelf and sobbed in the remorse he would never feel.

Great philosophers say that such bathyspheres of coruscating pain are the only avenue to true growth and original sight—of character. I have lost my credible compass—and I do not trust a single chamber of my heart anymore. I was conscious on the day he left that it was my last silence. That the progression of clouds and clocks around me were in the last quarter of shielding me from what I had to tell. In just a few more ticks and flutters, I'd have to call them all and meet them all and form it. How strange that people think of leaving and separation as emptiness—truly its solid figure is more ominous and imposing than any tangible fear on earth. It hovers around your skin like an inverted-rapist you wish would sink in and attack but will only touch lightly at your sorest spots. I'd love to be a dame about all this. To light cigarettes and salute mornings with flipped hair in ornate bathrobes and long skinny jeans. To lope like a bored lagoon into the dynamo gustatory institutions of New York and order "diet ice" with a straight face. But I am a tiny girl.

And yet........

My tiny life ended on February 6, 2005 and I didn't want to forget this married self, my only self, in lieu of a future, a freedom, or another married self. What was my lexis of cool again? Paragons of endless glamour, glamazons of mind and manner. I needed to decorate his departure with striations of Shinto sensibility. To remember that there are spirits in all things--even in divorces from men one never should have given a second glance toward.

Throughout the cavernous ruins of my life the smell of intrepid innocence has permeated--all the way down to the celestine clouds of Lethe--and back up again, to the big-tent hypergravity of a woman I knew it had always been my destiny to be. To the realization that *I* was the artist in the room. It had always been *me*--all that time I was hero-worshipping him. I was the enchanted coral *en ville*. I was, well and truly, the confetti cannon, the Milanese excess, and the jocular scrum. What time had I, then, for exoplanets?

Looking at his life-defunct face my first thought was: how odd for a champion narcissist to die with so few teeth. Funny that. This is what decimation and divorce sound like. Mega analog. Oh so very *handy*.

Waiting: A Psalm
Charlotte Friedman

You cannot say I am not here.
I show up, sway and sing,
stand, sit. I bend
my knees, bow,
look up, look down, turn
towards the door
and wait.

You cannot say I am not here.
I show up—not empty but
hauling a week's worth
of world, weary,
worn, falling apart.
I ask, beg you
and wait.

You can say I am not here,
I have not shown up. It's true
I am holding onto the world
out there—a daughter's
anger, wife's misunderstanding,
mother's regret—that
and more.

I want to be empty, so
you might pour yourself
into me. Find the cracks,
crevices, places where I have broken
open. Like a salve, heal.
But then would I have created
you in my shape
and not allowed your own?
What if I don't recognize you?

Desire has colored
my words and thoughts.
Is that unseemly,
inappropriate,
to want?

Say what you want.
I'll listen and show up and shut up.
I'll open myself and the book,
feel my way into those
lettered spaces. Cradles.
Cradles that hold
the darkness.

Waiting
Shaun Anthony McMichael

On the edge of my seat,
I'm at a bus stop moment where I want to know
when my what's-next is going to come
and what it's going to be—
A humble coach rumbling me in no hurry
through a future of nodding off
and waking in fits and starts
if this is a bus stop? Or if it's a tarmac,
my tomorrow landing on me like a jumbo jet.

There's trembling. Movement? No,
the trembling is in me.

When, what, how long—
the W's go down this page and through my mind
like herringbones down the coat of Fate,
the figure who won't answer.

I scooch myself back
on this bus stop seat, more of a slab.
How do you make yourself at home on a cliff edge?
No more questions!
I dangle my feet over as I did over
the edge of the windowsill in my mother's house
while I waited for Dad to pick me up

and when I realized the time wasn't coming
when I'd get to decide when,
I closed my eyes,
deciding I'd tell him about all I saw inside—
a rainbow bus rounding the corner. It's joint,
an accordion making music in my mind.

The Regular
Kurt Olsson

He's Bill, that's all.
No one's sweet Will.
Certainly not Billy.

If anyone calls him William,
his mother or his accountant,
if he has either. He drinks

whatever's on tap,
nothing else. Never eats anything,
not even the popcorn

and it's free. If he talks,
he smiles, embarrassed
or a mite proud he's got

an angle his own to share.
When he gives up
his barstool at last call, he stands

stock-still a few seconds,
maybe more. Shuts both eyes,
as if he needs the world

to settle inside him
or must count to make sure
his four limbs are his

and still with him. Then
he steps out into the same night
that waits for us all.

Charlie Parker
Sekani Johnson

it's that groove, it's that bebop.
it's that be duh de ya boh waiy eeeeeeyyyaaaaa
duwaaaaaayyyy, you know?
that makes your hand stretch slow across your face pulling at
your bottom lip.
watch them salivate in pools begging to satiate their Curiosity,
show them what the mirror has gifted you.
it's the drum solo coming down to the final bars
—the heavy click rrrrrr clack, boo pap k't tsss, that boom badoom
bap
that makes your whole being come up to the eggshell lining of
your skull,
floating you haphazardly to ascension. the climax that rolls out in
curtains of rhythm,
oh! that swing of your body across lines of hesitation and
exploding petals, littering the open bells.
keep time with it, stroke your syncopation baby, bounce with it on
the tops of your fingerprints.
be wrong, play that note sweet, play that note loud, play that
note like it owes you something,
play it like God is on the other line of the phone. call it a revision
of the art.
let them cut the mic, dim the lights. bellow loud and
shake sequins made from broken glass, echo all that is inside
you.
gravity wades in the waves of your pitch.
even if you are ignored, you are heard.
they don't have to look, they don't have to make time to forget
the performance.
no critic sailing their comments through microscopes,
whispering from high balconies towards brass necks crouched in
open pits,
has been able to cock a head up towards Curiosity and dribble

out
a response. they don't know to hold such things,
gripping the trunk like an axe when it is a weighted lance.
but you have rehearsed this moment, staring down fevered
Anticipation
as it gurgles through dark walls of chaste silence. show them
how to hold and whirl your bow
etched with chasms of alchemy: ornate brass and silver or
shedding iron or taped ceramic.
show off the black art of twisting wisps of starlight and melting
tears of gels into gold. teach them what
greater things you can conjure without props. show off. no
applause is better than always waiting for
your cue. this band ain't never had a conductor baby. show off.

Late Hour
Naomi Bess Leimsider

There is still plenty of sheer chance left for me in the world. In a universe dying
to be born, even a false form can be a future home. Maybe statistics mean little
in the face of so much space.

How I long for a body! Just to hold slippery organic matter in my hands, feel it
do its slipping, pulsing, thumping thing. Lungs up. Hips long. Abdomen heavy, low.
Notice breath. Notice bones. Assess stress. Assess balance. Big tolerance for spiking temperature, the flow of change, many kinds of pain.

Take me back to the energy of the beginning. Remember the solid structure of all
those days of stunning beauty one after the other. Reach back and time curves. Reveal
that last year was the last year I knew anything at all. Remind me of what's going on
beyond a hard no for the future, equations that won't work in my favor. It could still
go either way. This is how it is: the past always falls away.

I've lost my mind before. The intimate connection with the fabric of my space is delicate, porous, but I'm in this for the long haul. I am serious, but there's been significant restriction here. At this late hour, when, finally, consent is freely given, my default is still to be so, so
quiet, and also refuse to listen. It seems I need to walk around the world before the lesson
comes clear: there is loss, but I am right here.

Perhaps I will not last long enough to see this through. Every

night I take off my face
and see what can be salvaged, what remains. In all probability,
the multiple organs and
strings of muscular things that make up this mostly functioning
form are past the point
of practice. So I go incognito: the trick is to blend better, so no
one can see you.

I squeeze into a small pocket of time in this space between
stops. Not a second spared,
not a minute wasted. The last available universe ups the ante;
makes me work for it.

Widow at Thanksgiving
Kristin Zimet

I'm in for it. Trapped
in the holidays. I pace,
a polar bear in Central Park,
encased in useless fat and fur,
crossing my cell, this cement
neverground, this tepid pool,
this shrunk alien geography.
The heat, the noise, the glare.
People watching how I pass
or don't for normal, laughing,
moving on to celebrations in
new houses, big exhibits,
other species in their element.

A certain number, now, of steps
and turns and steps might take
or never take me back to thick
ice that supports my weight,
that wind-licked expanse,
that bracing cold for which
my heat was made. Go.
My nails gouge the floor,
my paws keep slapping, it's
a form of faith I practice.
A mate waits for me, bulk
invisible against the snow.
North in a perfect night.

Jolly Christmas
Marah Reinoso Vega

December 25th is finally here.

At nine in the morning, I have my hot cocoa cooling, my "Santa Baby" song playing, and my red dress on. For the first time in my life—twenty-two years—I'm going to celebrate Christmas. I know what to expect because I've seen it in the movies.

Yearly, I've constructed Christmas in my head with what I've learned from films. And I'm not talking about those flicks in which people want to escape the holiday tradition to go to the beach or get drunk somewhere, that's ludicrous. When I imagine this special occasion, I see a wide-smile-family decorating a real pine tree, children opening presents, a table set with a feast like those shown in seasonal magazines, and everyone gathered around the fireplace wearing a Santa hat and talking merrily while listening to carols and eating dessert.

The last image is bleary because I don't know what a Christmas dessert is like, but I imagine it's sweetlicious.

But listen, it's not that I had a sad childhood or that my parents didn't want to celebrate la Navidad, it's that the Cuban government didn't allow it for political and economic reasons. Reasons I won't bore you with.

When I turned five however, my Spanish-born-Catholic grandparents tried to teach me about baby Jesus and Christmas, and grandma gave me a wonderful dollhouse that she, herself, had played with as child. She had kept it in excellent condition for her future daughter, but when her daughter didn't like to play with dolls, she saved it for her future granddaughter—me.

The following year, my Cuban grandma decided that she, too, wanted to give me Christmas, and somehow (certainly illegally) bought a living turkey five days before the festivity.

On the morning of December 24, Cuban grandma announced that we would be having turkey for dinner. Without warning, she grabbed the neck of the bird and twisted and twisted and twisted, and feathers levitated around us, and I can't remember if the creature made a sound because my screams deafened my ears.

And then, she chopped its head off.

I ran directionless until my dad captured me and took me away from the house until dinnertime. So, I know what turkey meat tastes like.

Later, my parents agreed that celebrating Christmas was dangerous, not because of the violent-death-of-a-bird-trauma I still carry, but because if I had mentioned "turkey," "gift," or "baby Jesus" at school, I would have been bullied by teachers and peers and my family would have been reprimanded by co-workers and neighbors.

Thus, the holiday season became a collage of plagiarized images in my head.

Then, at age twenty, I left home and moved to Dubai for work and freedom of festivities—little did I know Emiratis didn't celebrate Christmas either.

It's been two years since I made the move, but that doesn't matter now, for I'm about to go to my friend's house to experience "the most wonderful time of the year" with her family and a handful of acquaintances. I imagine English people are experts at fulfilling such traditions.

Earlier today, a text message confirmed that Secret Santa would begin at eleven. I want to get there earlier because my British peeps ("peeps" being my newest English word) are always punctual.

My friend's parents came to the United Arab Emirates back when rules were strict and salaries bountiful. They live in a seven-bedroom-eight-bathroom-two-story-villa. As I arrive, I count fifteen people of various ages gathered in the living room with an alcoholic beverage in their hand. There is no fireplace. There are no children. There is an enormous artificial pine tree covered in expensive-looking ornaments that oddly enough complement the rest of the house décor: vintage furniture, buddhas, African masks, Indian tapestries, Persian carpets, khanjars—curved daggers from Oman—and fancy knickknacks.

A slender English gentleman in a crisp grey suit is smoking

apple-flavored shisha, and the sweet aroma blends in with the warm smell of roast meat and cinnamon candles.

I only know six people, but everyone greets me as if they've known me for years, and before I get a chance to place my gift under the tree, I'm holding a vodka-tonic-with-a-dash-of-lemon-juice in my hand and cheering to a "Merry Christmas!"

Alcohol is legal to have and consume at home for expats who possess a liquor license. Licenses must be approved by the Ministry of Interior and can only be given to non-Muslim UAE residents. The newer generation of expats rarely bothers to get permits because we've always had easy access to alcohol—just Uber to the corner where you'll find a hotel or mall with a bar indoors—but the older generation had to taxi a little farther, perhaps cross a bit of desert, to consume an alcoholic beverage in a male-dominated bar inside a business hotel.

So, they got into the habit of hoarding alcohol at home.

Gift exchange begins on time and soon turns into a frenzy. Everyone is opening their presents at the same time while making emoticon faces with the occasional "oh, thank you." My secret santa—a soft spoken lady wearing a green jumper with an embroidered poinsettia—gives me a medium-sized bag. Inside is a onesie—I'm a grown woman holding a onesie covered in tiny Rudolfs and expected to be delighted. I smile splendidly.

Soft 70s music the likes of "Stayin' Alive" by Bee Gees plays in the background.

After the gifting kissing and hugging, we sit at the dining table which has been lavishly set by a team of hired help—mostly Filipino expats who exit the house giggly.

My pictured banquet had a pillow-size turkey in it, but today's tangible menu consists of roast beef, sliced roast turkey, cranberry sauce, chestnut stuffing, pigs in a blanket, roast potatoes baked potatoes mashed potatoes, brussels sprouts, Yorkshire pudding, and gravy.

Everyone drinks their preferred alcoholic beverage accompanied by a glass of red wine (to go with the meat) and a champagne flute filled so that bubbles dance in the air as we toast and stare into each other's eyes (to avoid seven years of bad sex).

Table manners are a must. Both my grandmas taught me to eat everything on my plate. I wonder if that applies here.

"Sara, dear," calls the lady with the red bowler hat, "would you be so kind as to pass me the gravy?"

"Yes, of course." I answer with a Cuban accent that I only notice for the first time.

"Wonderful. Thank you." She pours gravy over her Yorkshire pudding and I tell myself to do the same when the viscous sauce comes around.

I try to remember what the medium-size fork is used for but soon realize that everyone is eating as if it was their last day on earth, and no one is paying attention to my medium-size fork.

So I feast.

As a rule, no one leaves the table until the last person is done eating. I'm on my third glass of wine. The man with ginger hair offers champagne.

Nearly three hours later, the host brings in the dessert (hear the ice cream truck tune in your head) mince pies, shortbread biscuits, warm plum pudding with brandy sauce, and trifle.

My eyes like what they see. My nose is pleased. My palate and tongue go to work.

The pudding is an acquired taste, says the palate.

The sweetness of the mince pies confuses me, but I eat them with gusto, says the tongue.

The feast ends with a digestif cherry liqueur.

Imminent, omnipresent lethargy.

Around five thirty, we're jolted back to life by the Adhan—the call to prayer that cuts through every home by means of a loudspeaker and a muezzin or crier. In Abu Dhabi, mosques are conveniently located on every block.

Instantly, my friend's boyfriend leaps out of his seat and replace the 70s music with Pop House.

We drink, play party games, play drinking games, smoke shisha, dance, try on onesies, nibble on leftovers, and nap in between. Every now and then, one or two people disappear into the second floor and reappear an hour later looking either rested or disheveled.

In the evening, the weather is pleasant at about 23°C or 75°F and the party moves to the terrace. My friend's parents and someone's else parents jump in the pool.

It's my turn to choose a drinking game. I recall the movies in my head and propose beer-pong. An Irish couple in their fifties swear they invented the game and join us to prove it. They lose, and drink, and argue they've won because the whole point is to drink.

Another couple, a petite French woman with coal-black hair and red lipstick, and her six-foot-plus British-Mauritian husband, announce they've been taking salsa lessons and change the music to Cuban.

They look at me.

I tell them I'm too full to move because if I say that I don't know how to dance, it will create confusion and disbelief followed by questions I won't know how to answer. Apparently, being Cuban and not knowing how to salsa is blasphemy, so I lie.

Every fifty-year-old starts to spin. "The best instructor," they say, "is a Lebanese guy who teaches at the Hilton." "If you're interested," they kindly continue, "his wife offers belly-dancing lessons for beginners; she's from Lithuania but speaks Spanish."

The couple's sons—one happy and overweight, the other skinny and high on hashish—are smoking Marlboro Red and taking turns to hit on the blonde with coconut-size breasts.

I hear a nice-looking couple in their forties tell the grey-suited man that they're "swingers." The blonde girl explains to me the meaning of "swinging."

A new English word is added to my vocabulary.

Someone's dad or friend or both, a gastroenterologist wearing a Rolex and shiny burgundy shoes (he works for a Sheikh he's not allowed to name) insists on putting his hand on my lower back.

I move away.

He comes close, again, and talks to me as if nothing, as if *that* wasn't his hand feeling my back. I tell him, "te voy a lanzar a la piscina," as if nothing, as if throwing him in the pool wasn't a big deal.

He gets it. The hand goes looking for a whisky glass to hold.

I try to think of traditional Christmases, but an inebriated spirit possesses me and I hear myself say: "I have an idea! Let's drink shots inside the pool!"

Although barely an idea, everyone applauds. Those wearing a swimsuit grab a bottle and jump in. The rest dip their feet in the blue water and hold a glass in each hand. This is not the Christmas that I had pictured, but it's an improvement from the frantic body of a turkey running without its head. And the mood is indeed merry.

I pour myself a shot of Baileys, seize the iPod, play "A Holy Jolly Christmas" and embrace the non-tradition while making a mental note: HOST THE NEXT CHRISTMAS.

A Winter Philosophy...
Gaylord Brewer

...of split beef shanks, heavy of marrow bone and white fat, dusted in flour

and seared in olive oil in your Dutch oven. Remove. Brown the diced onions

and rough-chopped garlic, lots of garlic, a treatise of garlic, then deglaze

with a generous pour of red wine, the rest of the bottle in generous

proposition. Stir in the beef stock, tomato paste, *bouquet garni* of thyme and

rosemary knotted by your own hand, bay leaf, and secret spoonfuls of

molasses for umami, adobo for fire. It's your life, and you live it once.

Generous grinds of pepper and salt. Taste. Trust the path you've chosen,

your sure premise. Return shanks to pot, bring to a boil.

Braise in the oven at a low temperature for three hours. That is, start early,

and be patient. Anticipation is itself a pleasure. The wheel of the cold day

turns. An inference of bare trees. A solitary cardinal at the feeder. A

childhood memory. The bemusing contradiction of whom you have become.

The good smells warming the house. Your shared and pleasant hunger.

These, the further arguments. An hour before dinner, the early night already

descended, add the parsnips, a single sliced carrot, more onion, and return

again to the oven. Patience. You are close now. Twenty minutes.

Stir in the
rinsed white beans, lovely pebbles of cannellini.

You know the rest. Make your case. Bowls and napkins, spoons, warm loaf of
bread. The candles lit, the summons that the moment has arrived. Stew in
the center of the table, and with a flourish the lid lifted, a conclusion of
steam, of rich fragrance, of feast, of hearty reckoning, as full an
understanding as you are ever likely to know.

January Burial
Patrick Hansel

I throw the blessings
of the day on the crisp
snow of our backyard garden:
coffee grounds, onion skins,
the stem of the last runted
squash we picked in November.
The remnants creak as they skid
across the sheen. Better
Homes and Gardens would crucify
us for the dark blotch polluting
the sea of pristine white. (Well,
maybe "crucify" is too strong
a word, an ancient method
of execution fetishized by
the professionally pious. Perhaps
"scorned" will suffice.) Scattered
are the figments of our daily
digestion; no perceived pattern
but loss. If the great star we spin
around each year appears today,
some of our departed gifts
may sink a bit into the melting.
Perhaps a rabbit will sniff out
the pile past midnight. But
eventually, each bit of
discarded plant flesh will be
redeemed by a practice older
than bone or eyes: the unburied
devoured, digested, dropped,
mixed with moldering soil,
a dark juicy pall of nutrients
to bless the riches buried deep:

some we will push into the soil
come May, some already waiting
to surprise, singing softly in the dark.

Hello Again
Eva M. Schlesinger

I see you from the bus and shout "hello" out the window. You're riding your sister's bike with the banana seat. "I'll call you when I get home," I yell. You nod, weaving in and out of traffic. You have the best hair flopping over your eyes.

Remember when we met a year ago on the bike path that loops through town? You squealed at our matching lime green jackets and said we were two peas in a pod. You introduced yourself by your initials—Y.M.—and said they stood for You and Me.

"Bea F.F.," I said. My hand, clasped between yours, felt at home.

Initially, you and I called each other every day; you ended with "love ya!" The past few months, when I've called you, you've said each time you were just about to call, and you signed off with, "Trust me, Dearest, you've given me enough to last a lifetime." Did you get my recent phone message: "Were you expecting me to call because the reason I didn't is I felt tired because I called you and if I call someone too much I get tired and I checked with myself and one part of me said call, and the other part of me said that *you* should."

The bus farts exhaust when it lets me off.

"Hel-lo," you pant into the phone.

"Can I come over?"

You say you have to go; your flowers are without water.

What about flowers that don't need water? If I got you some, we could stay on the phone like we used to, the phone clinging to my ear.

I bike to the nursery. A miniature spindly cactus, topped by a magenta flower, clutches my forearm with spiny arms as I walk to my bike. I cleverly use two tick-black Velcro straps to wrap the stem and tiny clay pot around my wrist, and pedal your way, my forearm prickled by little thorns.

Your voice that used to sing to me floats through your window. I drop my bike on your yellowing yard and flatten my face against the screen door.

You're giggling on the phone. The giggle-squeal you reserved for us. Giggle-squealing with a friend. Your eyes crinkle and your lips curve up so high they look pasted on. My arm is bleeding.

"Call 9-1-1." Blood drips, staining your Welcome mat.

The door pushes me aside as you stomp onto the porch, heat shimmering from the wooden boards. You swat air, as though to keep it from sticking to you. A frown of perspiration distorts your lips. I show you the little cactus, hugging my arm with its magenta smile.

"For you!" I beam.

Your heart-shaped nostrils shut fast, as if my gift smells like skunk cabbage. You tug and tug at the straps, then yank hard, Velcro screeching, as you grab the clay pot and hurl the cactus onto the grass. Clay shatters on my bike, slashing the flower smile into a scowling green gash. Spiky arms entangle with the wheels.

I put the broken cactus pieces in my shorts pocket. I bike home slowly. My wheels wobble and limp, tires deflated.

I speed dial your number.

You say you're drained from people showing up on your doorstep needing stuff.

"Traveling salesmen?"

The phone wails, disconnected.

I hit redial.

Now it's a new YM: You are always Missing.

Doesn't mean we won't talk again.

Wait For It
Mary Beth O'Connor

the punchline
the red light
the train
the first robin
dessert
the launch
break time
the ice cream truck
the bride
the test results
the next pain pill
the ambulance
some peace and quiet
the balloon to burst
the phone to stop ringing

fireflies
the tomatoes to ripen
the leaves to change
the song to end
the next episode
the kids to go back to school
this party to be over
the power to be restored
the reveal
the paycheck
morning
the other shoe
the first snowfall
the dog to come back
the game to begin
the commercial to end
the band to start playing

the baby to stop crying

the end
   of the chapter
   of the war
   of the epidemic
   of the affair
   of the world

When It Comes Hurtling Toward Us
Mary Beth O'Connor

i'll be wandering
down the railroad tracks
crossing over the creek,

wearing my sunglasses and
september hat—so caught up
in the bridge's rusty reddish glow

i can't be bothered to turn
or jump or lie down flat

when it hits, i'll have reached
the top of lick brook glen, where
i'll sit, imperceptible, just off the trail

and watch red-tailed hawks
ride the spiraling thermals
in the gorge just below

as the falls cascade
over ancient shale layers

late clouds will gather
and the sun fall
into its other life

Signs of the Time
Alice Friman

Everyone sooner or later flashes a sign
of what or who they are, the way
a dentist's setup on the frontier
hung out a massive tooth to alert
the illiterate, or how Destiny Fellowship
places a pew on the sidewalk in front
of its store-front church to advertise.

What else is the cross or star worn
around your neck? What means a tattoo,
a wedding ring, four-hundred dollar sneakers,
the snarky comment on your T-shirt?

The rioters who breached our Capitol
with flags and clubs were walking signs
egged on by a bigger one: a billboard
in a long red tie. You saw it, you were there:
an army of raging signs announcing
the coming storm, flaunting its numbers.

Your little bumper sticker won't be enough.

The Morning News
Karen Kilcup

April 2020

The peepers' sleigh bells are   white weight.
so's Santa, and all the
reindeer,   gone—
their lichen under ice they   too—
can't lick   through
(the climate's   changing)
while we indoor animals   play
with YouTube videos of cities   towns
and   wild:
gone   trimmed Welsh hedges,
mountain goats atop   howling in Tel Aviv,
jackals   Corsican boars,
feral   frolicking in Ahmedabad,
grey langurs   lumbering down a New Delhi
buffalo   highway.
In Santiago   a cougar climbs
a concrete wall.

Some images are fake,   but the world
can still discover something   real—
Punjabis see   the Himalayas;
in L.A. the sky is   blue—
and Times Square hosts   ghosts
of shoppers and clickers and   gawkers
gone home, the old order   restored,
or another   one
begun.

Along   my country road,
pines   groan and thrash
with spring   storms,
as we, mere mortals,   await
returning winter's   wild

July Frost
James William Gardner

Climax was a hot dusty place in summer. The tobacco fields seemed to exist in a perpetual brown haze born more of Heaven than of earth. Reverend Dooley said that most things were. So it was with Virginia Wray's baby, Elizabeth. She was a gift from God, the only one that Virginia Wray had ever truly known.

Tobacco had a certain surreal quality. Running through it was like pushing your way into a crowd. Leafy green arms reached out to touch you and slow you down. You had to step lightly lest you stumble and find yourself face down, sprawled out on the hard red earth, tripped and your chin bleeding. But when the time finally came and the trailers were loaded and Danville beckoned, the work was done and the man from R. J. Reynolds gladly bought everybody lunch. Then, like Easter morning, it started all over again.

"I do not envy others," said Virginia Wray, standing there in the Food Lion parking lot with Joanne Butler while the boy put the groceries in back. "We have a plenty and that's all you can ask." But, Elizabeth Wray was older now. She was all but grown up at fourteen. "Lord Honey, you're going to drive the men wild. Be careful. Know what you're getting into." Late at night she would stand in front of the mirror with just the table lamp on, naked and dance to please herself.

Down the Chatham Road were the Roops, Mister Claude Roop, his wife Wanda and their boy, Curtis. On his seventeenth birthday, Claude Roop gave his son a set of barbells so he could build himself up. Curtis Roop was planning to work the land like his father and it took strength for that. "Where in the devil is that boy when you need him?"

"He's lifting those infernal weights you got him, I bet," said Wanda Roop as she rinsed off tomatoes from the garden. "That boy is obsessed with his muscles. He ain't going to fit in his

Sunday suit if he keeps on."

"Well, I'll just have to get him a new one, I reckon."

The Roops were church people, Independent Baptists, serious minded and strict when it came to religion. Curtis Roop had read a chapter in the Bible every night before bed since the time that he was able to read. They weren't like Virginia Wray. She didn't believe in nothing but herself and she was raising her only daughter the same way. "That woman is out until all hours," Wanda Roop used to say about her only close neighbor. She often used the word "heathen" to describe Virginia Wray's doings. "That poor little girl, she's growing up just like her momma."

"She's an awful pretty little thing," said Claude Roop. "I seen her out hanging wash the other day when I drove by wearing nothing but a bathing suit, practically naked for all the world to see."

"I don't doubt it."

When school started that September, Elizabeth Wray and Curtis Roop rode the same bus. She was just starting high school. Curtis Roop was a senior. "I swear to the Lord, that girl is about the sexiest thing I believe I've ever seen," He told his friend Leon Spradlin when Elizabeth Wray climbed on the bus that first morning.

"You'd best stay away from that stuff," Leon Spradlin advised him, but Curtis Roop flexed his new muscles and Elizabeth Wray was quick to notice.

It wasn't long before he had stopped reading his Bible at night and was sneaking out to meet her after his folks were in bed asleep. "Lord Lizzy, I just got to have you. I can't stand it. You're all I think about."

"So have me," she told him.

The October moon looked like a silver dollar that night. Afterward, they started talking about their dreams, what they wanted to do, what they could do. This went on. "Let's just go," she said one night.

"Go where?"

"Let's go to Atlanta. I got an aunt there. We could stay with her."

"I can't just up and leave everything like that. I don't know nothing about Atlanta. That's three states away. What would we do? It's crazy talk."

"You don't really love me."

"Yes I do so, but you're just a kid."

"Is that what you think?" He felt her warm skin against his and he knew that it wasn't so. He had never loved anything so much.

"Momma would track us down. She'd tell the police and we'd be up shit creek. I might even go to jail."

"Atlanta ain't like here. There's people everywhere. No one will find us. We can take Momma's car."

"Lizzy, we can't steal your mother's car. Talk sense."

"Well, we can take the bus. I've got some money saved. We can skip school and catch the Greyhound bus at noon when it comes through Chatham."

"You're just pussy whipped," said Leon Spradlin. "That girl has got you all fucked up so you ain't thinking right. I told you to watch out."

"She's done spoke with her aunt Charlotte down there. She says it's okay with her if we come. She says she won't tell a living soul."

"You're out of your mind, Curtis."

They packed suitcases and hid them down by the Banister River Bridge. Then on Tuesday, they caught the southbound bus for Atlanta with three-hundred dollars between them. "Well, it's perfectly clear to me," said Sheriff Wilbur Bates two days later. "Those two youngins have run off together. Lord knows where."

"My son is a good boy," said Wanda Roop tearfully. "That darn little Jezebel has done corrupted his mind. I blame the mother. She's the one. Just look at the example she's set, out all night, running around, probably sleeping with God knows who all."

"Well, we'll get the state police on it. We'll find them."

Atlanta Georgia stood against the horizon like the city of Oz. It stretched on and on and on, people and cars and buildings everywhere you looked, people from everywhere, talking all kinds of languages. It wasn't old like Climax or Chatham. That was the past. This was the future. It was a place where no one knew you and no one cared to know. There didn't seem to be any place for God, no reason or need for Him at all.

Charlotte Tinsley's apartment was on the ninth floor. Curtis Roop had never been so high. "Well, I'll say one thing for him Honey, he's mighty good looking. Y'all can have the back bedroom. After you get cleaned up and rested we'll go get something good to eat and figure out what we need to do next."

Roswell was a happy seeming place. Everybody hurried by smiling. Elizabeth Wray wore one of her aunt's dresses, a short black dress that showed off her legs and made her look twenty. "Lord Lizzy, you're incredible," said Curtis Roop, amazed at the transformation. Looking at her made everything seem possible. They ate shrimp outside along the sidewalk and there was music in the air. He noticed other men looking at her and it made him proud.

The fantasy lasted almost a week. Then, on a rainy Saturday morning there was a knock at the door. It was the cops, two men in suits and they took them back home to Climax in a police van. No one said anything much on the drive back. It felt like being pushed into a hole. Elizabeth Wray held her lover's hand and watched the lights go by. Had it all been a dream?

Nobody pressed any charges. Curtis Roop and Elizabeth Wray returned to school and it was all kept quiet. But, to them, things were never like they were before. Claude Roop put a new lock on the back door and after awhile it came time for the tobacco seedlings to be stuck in the ground again. Curtis Roop went to sleep in the same little bed, in the same little room and waited in vain for the memory to go away, but he didn't bother reading his Bible anymore. He would just close his eyes until he floated off like innocence, like leaves on the Banister River.

Another Lockdown
Rohan Buettel

Each prosaic day a scurry from one
activity to another — now curtailed;
and time off for good behaviour is time
not spent in meetings or wasted on detail.
Relaxing with morning news and coffee,
a liberation from the daily grind,
the pestle no longer pounds the mortar,
all commitments ground, tearing ties that bind.
I start to appreciate the pleasure
of slowing down, a slave to busy days
freed from shackles by another lockdown
to holiday at home safe from the blaze.
Until thinking of coming months unplanned,
I begin to sink in quickening sands.

Office Hours, Zoom
Marisa P. Clark

Laptop's on and angled to show
the stippled ceiling, off-white wall, the air
conditioning grate above the door,
and my tousled crown of graying hair. I pass

the time reading, and between poems, I study
the items littering my desk. A green pen
that inks thick lines. A blue saucer freckled
with pepper and salt from breakfast

yesterday. Plasticware, unopened, and two
unused tan paper napkins. Fingernail
clippers. Textbook on a haphazard stack
of pages scrawled with lesson plans, arrows,

and questions for discussion. Windex
multisurface cleaner, with vinegar—no recollection
what I cleaned, if anything. A parrot perch,
no parrot perched. Just out the window,

six pygmy nuthatches peck the dying flowers
on the vitex tree, then fly on. Propped
on the sill behind a row of painted stones,
an oracle card provokes: I HONOR HOW

I WANT TO FEEL. And there's the wad
of olive drab, the shirt I wrested from the jaws
of my bored dogs during class—I never stopped teaching
that grid of black rectangles with white printed

names, the occasional avatar, my exhausted face.
It's ruined now—holes bitten in the linen. Zoom

used to mean much more than just close focus.
Regardless--

if anyone cares to meet, I'm here.

44

A Different Body
Erika B. Girard

I do not see the sky.
I do not see the clouds with their whitish/grayish tint.
Only cement. Approaching at a ridiculous speed.

Time slows as it usually does
when one is freefalling through a city that only sleeps
on park benches and magazine covers.
When the tease of freedom lasts but a moment
before reality hits
and your fall is no longer evitable.
When gravity means you won't need to worry about
tomorrow
because, expectorated from the highest point in the city,
you no longer have that option.

I wonder what it's like to fall
if you wear a parachute
like, for fun or something. Is it?

I cannot brace myself any more than I dare hope
the splatter on the sidewalk will be easy to clean up
because I think about others before myself
except I forgot for this.
Others will not mind my disappearance
until they need to scrape what remains.

Did I mean to fall?
I wonder
but it's too late to come up with the right answer
I was pushed, I remember
I was pushed but I let myself be pushed
and that's not easy to reconcile.
I remind myself it doesn't matter no—
And suddenly I am a grease spot on the pavement.

The world has been replaced by blue.
Because that is all I can see now.

And I hear from high above me a curse of disappointment
that I, invisible to the naked eye,
did not, in fact, peg any poor passersby.

Summary as a Poem Figuring Itself Out
Chinua Ezenwa-Ohaeto

In Igbo, the word for cup is iko.
And I ask: when will my iko ever be fully full?
It is in E equals M C squared that I understood
how we, sometimes, can flavour too dark.
No one teaches how to handle shortcomings.
I want to understand the designs of living and crossing.
I don't want the men inside of me screaming dust.
I keep bumping into myself
trying to find touch, trying to
seek something that is not an apology.

The Empty Nest
Alice Friman

All June, a nature show played itself out
outside our kitchen window—birds

hatching, feeding. We, nose-pressed,
kept a lookout for snakes, for they were

our birds—baby-new tenants of the world.
We worried they weren't being fed enough.

Where's Mother, we demanded of an empty sky.
Or Dad—isn't he supposed to help? We turned

our chairs at the table to track them as
we ate, as if the future of those four fluffs

depended on our two eyes. When they fledged—
flapping furious to muscle up their stubby wings—

we cheered them on. But when they left,
as they were wont to do, we were lost in a fog

of now-what, like parents facing a vacant
room—posters down, photos all boxed up.

Why that effect? We'd seen birds before,
watched them come and go. Yet for weeks,

we kept our vigil, hoping they'd return
for old times' sake, or at least (our joke) for

Mother's cooking. But I wonder. Now that
we're back to pass-the-salt and would-you-

care-for-more-salad, what were we so
empty for, hungry for, that needed to be fed?

49

Love Story
Susan Phillips

She was totally enthralled by him. That's how she described her feelings to her friends. He was dreamy to look at—tall, dark and handsome. He was smart, he was cute, he had a good paying steady job. He knew how to sail and had borrowed his parents' boat on sunny days and moonlit evenings to take her all around Boston Harbor. He was everything she wanted.

He loved her wide smile and upbeat personality. He loved that she enjoyed all the dates he planned so carefully—skating on Frog Pond, exploring the Harbor Islands, taking the train to Rockport then walking to Gloucester and taking a train home, walking on both sides of the Charles River. She often brought her camera along and he loved how she concentrated as she framed and shot photographs. When she was especially focused on capturing an image she seemed to forget he was there. He loved her enthusiasm—for photography, for the art museums they visited, for every new restaurant they found and for him.

She'd spent too many Valentine's Days alone or disappointed. There was the boyfriend who broke up with her on February 12 and another who called VD a Hallmark holiday and didn't even send her a card. One old flame had complained about the cost of the Valentine's Day special all during dinner and another claimed to have forgotten the date. He also forgot her birthday, so one day she forgot to call him back and never saw him again. But Dave remembered everything—the date they met, their first kiss, the first present she gave him. And he had promised her a special Valentine's Day this year. At times he seemed to avoid talking about things—analyzing their relationship in long heart to hearts. Maybe they didn't need to. Maybe he would start saying all she needed to hear.

He made dinner reservations a month in advance. He wanted to be sure he got a table with the best view at the Top of the Hub restaurant. They would look out the window and plan all the places they'd visit in the coming months. He took his best suit to the dry cleaners and went to the florist a week before to pick out a vase they would deliver to the restaurant, filled with a dozen long-stemmed red roses. He wanted everything to be perfect because she was perfect. They agreed on every topic they discussed. They never quarreled.

Along with most of the women in the office she left work early on Valentine's Day. Their boss smiled and shook his head. They'd probably waste hours the next day swapping stories about what they'd done, but all would be calm again the day after. She took a long bubble bath, then studied every good dress in her closet. Too long, too short, too tight, too loose. She fingered the material of the ones not rejected—too heavy, too flimsy. She finally decided on the deep purple velvet which hid all her figure flaws and a pair of red high heels. She wouldn't have to walk far. He would drive and not complain when he paid for parking. She pulled out a red velvet cloak she'd owned for years. It wasn't warm enough, but she wouldn't be outside too long.

He had laid out his clothes before he left for work and was ready in half an hour. He had everything, including a small velvet covered box.

The evening was magical—they both felt it. They smiled and laughed, shared their entrees and declared the wine perfect. She had been ready when he picked her up. He'd appreciated not having to wait the usual fifteen minutes as she dithered around, looked for things she'd forgotten, changed her shoes or handbag. As he talked about the future she hoped that he would be willing to have emotional talks where they could share their secret hopes and dreams. Was he ever a bit impatient when she wanted to talk about their relationship?

When they were halfway through the chocolate mousse he reached across the table and took her hand. "You know how I feel about you," he said. "You know I love you." He took the box out of his pocket and opened it. "I want to spend every day with you. Will you marry me?"

She looked up into his eyes, down at the diamond ring and up again. "I, I don't know," she said. "I have to think about it."

You shouldn't have to think about it, he wanted to yell at her. You should know, as I do. You should say yes right now.

A crowded restaurant on Valentine's Day was not the place where she could question him the way she wanted to—would he be willing to open himself more, to laying his soul bare?

Follow your heart, he thought, and let your head pick up the pieces. Don't you love me?

They married the next year—but not each other.

Waiting for Food
Jo Angela Edwins

If the dingy white curtain
bordered in blue flowers
didn't robe the window
of my galley kitchen,
the child I hear playing
in the yard next door
might catch a glimpse
of me leaning on the counter
reading poems in a thin book
while I await the incubation
of a margherita pizza
and sip a glass of wine.
If I were lithe and clothed
in a breezy summer dress
instead of hunched and wearing
an old T-shirt, older shorts,
she might get the notion
that the life of a teacher
home alone in July
were glamorous.
But I am aging. I limp.
I go days without talking
to a soul. I do not own
a single summer dress.
I still eat what's delicious,
though slightly less these days.
And that curtain always hangs,
hiding the mediocrity
of my every shuffling step.
The only thing, besides the wine,
is the poetry. Oh God,
the poetry I read
by people I've never met

who gently extract the beauty
of dead flies, grocery carts,
botched Nativity scenes
in which Jesus is nothing more
than dry kindling draped in duck cloth,
and perhaps that's all we need
to save us in this world—
pink cotton and a stick
that any moment could catch fire,
a child outside a window
playing games of invention,
ignoring the lonesome people
stuck indoors, waiting for food,
wishing they were more
than the beautiful, ordinary
humans that they are.

In the Flesh
Louise Wilford

From the gloom of your nose to the passport smile,
you're concealed in plain sight.
Online, your courage is irreverence –
you control the edge the world sees.

But when we talk, alone, in the sleepless hours,
connected by a mobile mast somewhere
out on the hills that lie between us,
your voice is rough as water falling over rocks –

much deeper than I guessed. Your words
drift from cool to hot, an electric wire
that flames against my ear. Your talk is woven
of folktales – the forested landscapes of your youth.

I feel your laughter in my veins.
When we meet, will I know you still?
Will you smell of grass and clay, of the trees
you climb, and the stone walls you build,

of the wind rattling through reeds?
Will your face be puckered with squinting
at poems, skin coarsened by outdoor life, pale eyes
narrowed from staring at the clouds?

I know the shape you make in the world.
I might not know your scent, your flesh –
but I know your midnight voice, the maskless dreams
that hold you tight when you cannot sleep.

Lonely Hinges
Eric Chiles

They're still stifled in their plastic wrappers
just waiting for when they can complete
themselves in opening and closing,
lubricated and swinging as good shiny
hinges should. The door knob, lock set,
too, want to turn and latch, but alas,
there's no door, ordered months ago,
but undelivered because of the pandemic.
If they could cry in their unfulfilled
loneliness, they'd rust. Instead they gather
dust on the workbench just like the pet
door and tools - chisel, drill, jigsaw, bits
- all set out like groomsmen, bridesmaids
for a marriage to close that cold void
covered by blankets to save some heat.
The cat doesn't mind; it's easier to push
past a blanket to get to the litter box
than learn how to navigate a pet door
which makes me worry about a stained
rug when that time comes which Marissa,
the sales associate, assures me surely will
arrive eventually, someday - it changes every
week she says when she calls the vendor
for an update - her voice softening, cracking
when I mention all that lonely hardware.

Making Room
Elise Chadwick

Already our home is a museum of cast-aways
and redundancies too precious for Goodwill.
Take the white Staffordshire dogs she says,
so we do.

Or the Grosz charcoal drawing,
legless specter on her bedroom wall.
I don't even know it's there,
so we bring it home too.

What do I need them for? she asks
about etched water glasses,
ornate covered serving dishes
before they migrate to my buffet
giving her cabinets room
to breath.

But today when she says
Buy something that will remind you of me
I sense she has transcended,
from unburdening and bequeathing
to the realm of anticipation
where the purpose is to clear
a space in my heart
a waiting room ready
for my grief
when she is gone.

Rum Raisin
Rachel Kim Raczka

Inside the Ice Cream Shop of Dreams, April Meters was out of Rum Raisin.

It was a pity. But no one really likes rum raisin. She replaced it with a flavor she called Inspiration, a slapdash pistachio and nougat ice cream made with leftover ingredients that she thought deserved a cheeky name.

"Give me two scoops of that green one," said her favorite customer, Martin Cameron, an elderly writer who came in to suck his pen and stare out of the front windows every day at noon.

She shoveled two creamy mounds into a red paper cup and handed him a tiny spoon.

"No refunds if it's bad," she said with a grin.

"How could it be?" he said. He swirled the velvety neon butter and took a bite.

"Delicious," he proclaimed

April hung a sign on the door – *Now Serving Inspiration* – rather pleased with her cleverness. Martin and his quickly filling notebook made an excellent window display.

"I'd like another," he said, his fingers still sticky with ink and cream. April happily obliged, giving him a sundae this time, topped with dollops of whipping cream and cherries. Martin squealed in delight, dropping a bill on the counter before retaining his spot by the front windows, scribbling away.

The shop received a good amount of foot traffic from the local university students who came by for a single scoop, no toppings, no tip.

"Is that like a Live Laugh Love thing?" one student said flatly while their fingers skidded across their phone screen.

April shrugged. "It's whatever you want it to be."

The student looked up just long enough to roll their eyes. "Fine. One scoop in a cup. No extras."

April noticed the translucent red and purple rings that framed their hollow cheekbones and battered and chewed cuticles. She sprinkled a handful of chopped nuts, the closest thing to nutritious she admittedly had, over the ice cream and handed it over.

"On the house," she said in a hushed tone. The student's eyes fluttered once behind their glasses before they were gone.

The new flavor, it transpired, was a hit. Students lined the walls, pushing their crinkled five-dollar bills her way, ordering that weird green one, and hovering far too long after it had melted.

The little shop was chattering and claustrophobic with the rhythmic scraping of chairs and tongues, as April had always pictured it. They said "thank you" on their way out the door. Some even learned her name, waving their hands and adding, "See you next time, April!"

"Until tomorrow," said Martin with a wink. "This one's a winner," he added, pointing his notebook toward the spoil of empty cups and spoons in the trash can.

April counted the bills – which generously compensated for her one charity scoop – and sat back, hugging the empty tub of Inspiration. She scraped the final frozen nougat from the bottom and popped it in her mouth. It really was sensational.

* * *

The next morning April arrived with a wooden crate of fresh cherries, which she pitted and smashed into a sweet cream base swished with bittersweet chocolate. She called it Promises, for the kindly fruit stall owner who always saved her the bruised pickings from the day before. Not good enough for social-media perfect parfaits, but ideal for ice cream.

"Have any more of that green stuff?" The student from the day before appeared seconds after she switched her sign to Open.

"I don't. One-time only," she said. The student let out a long, exasperated sigh, fogging the front of their glasses. "But I have this new one. You can be my first taster."

The door's chime twinkled as she scooped Promises into a cup and handed it to the student. Martin tipped his hat at her and dumped his notepads – now several, with a box of backup pens – onto the front table.

"What about the nuts?" the student said, taking the cup greedily.

"$3," April replied. The student let out another exhaustive huff and dropped the dollar bills and a pocketful of quarters onto the counter. No tip.

Martin was also disappointed Inspiration did not return, but begrudgingly ordered a double-scoop of Promises. "First no rum raisin, and now this," he said and April laughed.

Word must have spread that Inspiration was sold out, because the little shop remained quiet for the next hour or so. She scribbled out a new sign – *Promises for Sale* – and plopped it in the window next to Martin who was back to wistfully twisting his pen between his fingers.

"How's the great American novel going?" she said.

"Seems like it escaped me," Martin said regretfully. "But soon. It's coming soon."

April was filling her shakers with sprinkles when the door jangled again.

"Hello, old friend!" She heard Martin exclaim. The clack-clack-clack of heels shattered across her checkerboard floors.

"What can I get you—" April dropped her jar of sprinkles, freckling the ground with rainbow shots. A cow's pink marshmallow-y nose poked the glass protector before it let out of a great, guttural moo.

The thought that protesters to Big Dairy's agenda had gone too far crossed April's mind but she never was one to turn away a (potentially) paying customer.

"What can I get you?" she politely repeated. The cow nodded its mighty head toward the front sign. April scooped a hefty trough of Promises and added a spray of golden sprinkles and a split banana.

"Put it on my tab," said Martin, patting the space beside him in the front window. April gently placed the ice cream sundae atop the cow's back before it gracefully made its way over.

"Hello," said a wobbly voice. April looked around unable to locate its source.

Two fuzzy tennis balls bounced eagerly. She frowned.

"Two servings of Promises, please," they said, undeterred.

April filled two shot glass-size cups, typically reserved for her canine-safe desserts, and added small dollops of whipped cream.

"I am not sure what to charge you for this," she began but the tennis balls had dropped a $10 bill onto the counter. She sat the two capfuls of Promises on a high-top table and tried not to stare as they ping-ponged between them.

The door continued to clang, a gaggle of students wishing to try Promises, something their friend heard from a friend who saw it on Instagram. April filled the little red cups with pink swirls and watched as they devoured them and the tennis balls rolled out.

The remaining scoops of Promises were sold to the following: a flirtatious astronaut (whipped topping, extra fudge), a well-lubricated wine-and-book club (double cherries, please), a pair of dormice (with caramel drizzle in cones the size of thimbles), four shooting stars (one cup, four spoons), a divine horticulturalist on her way to a date (a double-scoop with crumbled brittle to soothe the nerves), an empty soda can (filled to the brim), and three dozen or so students she recognized from the day before.

April counted her overflowing till as Martin and his bovine friend gathered their belongings and bid her adieu for the day. The cow's servings of Promises alone allowed her to break even.

"Tomorrow," Martin said. The cow mooed.

April smiled and nodded her head.

* * *

The Ice Cream Shop of Dreams added Promises and Inspiration to their regular menu, permanently replacing Rum Raisin and Grasshopper, which, let's be honest, no one ever ordered anyway. April hired a new scooper to help keep up with the demand, the surly student from the other day. They matched the energy of the student population, menacingly tapping their fingers against the tip jar when each stepped up to pay. All they asked in return was unlimited free scoops on their break, which April was happy to oblige.

"I'm sick of Promises," one returning customer, a lumpy skein of mulberry yarn, whined. "I want something new."

"Then go somewhere else," said the student, carefully packing a waffle cone with the frozen pink confection.

Martin cackled from his perch in the front window, a stack of empty cups of Inspiration next to him. But April remained deep in thought, her eyes lingering on the line out the door.

"What kind of flavor would you want?" she asked the yarn.

The yarn twiddled its threads for a moment. "Something soothing, I think."

"I'll see what I can do," she said.

The student held out their hand, "Four dollars. Cash only."

April spent night after night watching her concoctions churn and churn. A salted caramel popcorn flavor called Comfort flew out of the freezer so fast she could hardly keep up. The yarn skein returned every day following, gratefully twisting over the tip jar. The horticulturalist ordered a gallon of Confidence, a new blueberry ice cream with thick streaks of cheesecake, and asked if she could place a hold for weekly replenishments. A pastel rainbow-colored gelato, inspired by April's favorite lassi flavors, was named Genius. It sold out before she could add it to the sign, courtesy of the army of tooting woodwinds that cha-cha-ed through the shop.

Agility and Commitment, two tart, sparkling citrus sorbets, became a popular combination. The university students, who now stretched the afternoon-to-evening line down the sidewalk, liked to pour cans of energy drinks onto their scoops. Speedily slurping pale orange slush down and posting their brain freeze on social media.

"One last scoop of Inspiration," said Martin, hustling up to the countertop, four disjointed notebooks nestled into his armpit. "And maybe a small dollop of Genius, just for kicks."

April plopped the cup on the counter and wiped her brow. "It's on the house, Martin."

Martin dropped his bills into the tip jar and looked up. His face drooped. "April, you look horrible. What's wrong?"

April hated nothing more than men who felt it was OK to gauge a woman's emotional status based on her appearance. But it was Martin. And it was Saturday.

"Nothing," she said, forcing a weak smile.

Customers knocked on the front window, attempting to catch her attention. The student, who was eating a cone with one hand, broom in the other, jerked their head toward the Closed sign. The customers pounded and pouted and April had to look away, shushing her guilt over their ice cream-less nights.

"I feel bad," she said.

"Don't," said Martin. He patted her hand and left out the backdoor. "Save me a pint of Inspiration tomorrow?"

April began to sleep in the ice cream shop. She liked to watch the machines as they churned, whirls of sweet dreams. They hummed, merrily, steadily, like passing ships, a gentle reminder that April had the gift of making someone's day. Even if it took all night.

April awoke to a swarm of customers at the front windows — honeybees and ballerinas, the tenured faculty of the English department, four Persian cats, and a nimbus cloud that appeared on the verge of rain. She rubbed her dry eyes and unlocked the door.

"I'm not ready for customers yet, but you can wait in here," she said as they flooded the shop.

When the student appeared an hour later, April handed them two scoops. "All hands on deck," she said. The student understood the assignment, delivering cup after cup of Commitment to the junior soccer league that just arrived.

Business was booming, raucous and exhausting. But April loved to watch the lines unfold, and her ice creams to twirl in their machines overnight. She dreamed of the love affairs and first recitals and new shoes and end to finals weeks that her creations would celebrate. She liked to think there was a little sparkle in their eyes (or whatever) when it was announced they were heading to the Ice Cream Shop of Dreams. Or maybe even when they said April, the owner.

April was hanging a new sign outside the window, when the

new flavors became too long to list. She had added Gusto, Victory, Compassion, and Hope — and two frozen yogurts, Values and Perseverance. All very popular.

"Hello there," said a familiar voice. Martin, holding a plastic tote, tipped his hat her way. April hadn't seen him in weeks — and she most certainly had never seen him outside of the shop.

"Martin! Where have you been?" She gave him a hug. She couldn't help it.

"Oh," Martin said sheepishly. "I hope you don't mind." He tugged at the bodega bag and pulled out one of the several boxes inside. It had a picture of a pasty green popsicle and a grand flourish of letters: Inspiration.

"How can this be?" April said. "This is mine. It's my creation."

"It's a bit cheaper," Martin said. "And at the rate I was going… I couldn't afford to keep up."

"But it's not as good as mine," April said defensively. "And it's not as good as Rum Raisin."

"No," Martin said. "But it does the trick."

He smiled awkwardly and patted her hand. Tucking the box back into his bag and continuing down the sidewalk to the awaiting cow on the street corner.

Clancy's
William Torphy

Shaun sits on the bar stool tapping his foot along with his phone. The man is late. He shouldn't have agreed to meet him. He's beginning to regret he ever began that web search.

He was surprised the man responded to his email: "Nice to here from you. Maybe we can meat sometime." He doesn't know what to make of the misspellings. Weird if they're intentional, pathetic if not. Never mind the asinine Betty Boop emoji that makes no sense, unless it's some readymade reference to the one person they have in common. He hasn't told her about his online sleuthing, certainly not about this meeting

The man suggested Clancy's. "It's my old hangout," he declared with a hint of nostalgia. The bar is a real dive. Too derelict to be retro, a holdout from downtown San Francisco's rougher past. It's days are definitely numbered, he thinks, squeezed on one side by a gleaming office tower, assaulted on the other by an Apple store. Everything here destined for landfill—the rusted bar stools with their battered, ass-pinching leatherette seats, the sticky linoleum flooring, the fake oak panelling encrusted with a century's worth of cigarette smoke.

He takes a sip at his Guinness, and as if on cue a cockroach skitters across the etched top of the bar and disappears down on the other side. His phone pings, breaking the bar's pall of silence. A text from his friend Brandon: *We still on?* They've planned to meet later at Martuni's before going to a new club South of Market. His fingers perform a swift dance. *Meeting someone.* Another ping moments later. *Wha fuck?!!* He taps out, *See u 6*, hits send. He's never mentioned this man to Brandon, not to any of his friends.

It might actually be a relief if the bastard doesn't show. No difficult questions to ask, no bullshit excuses to hear. He'll be able to hit delete and write-off the fucker for the rest of his life.

He stares into the hazy mirror behind the bar, his sandy hair and fair complexion glowing under a ceiling light, and steals a glance at the two customers hunched over their bourbons like hapless vultures. The fucking definition of forlorn, their faces flaccid, ghosted into white as if they haven't stepped outside of Clancy's in years. The man in the cheap grey suit raises a finger to request a refill, and when the bartender complies, shoots him a thumbs-up for no apparent reason other than to prove he can muster nonverbal communication. The bar's second denizen of the dark, a comb-over plastered against his skull, listlessly raises a finger too, as if he's been prodded awake from dormancy.

Odds are that the man he's meeting is a sad ruin like them. Images of an unfortunate future, of some screwed-up fate he believes only happens to other people—poverty and loneliness—cunningly takes roost in his head once again, but he quickly dismisses them. He's twenty-seven, after all, has a great job with Google, rents a cool apartment in the Mission and is skimming off the cream of earthly existence.

But shadows from the past always seem to lurk, phantoms that make him feel like a needy kid, the boy who undeservedly held himself responsible for his father's disappearance, for his mother's silent days in bed and nights tearing through the house raging against men in general and his father in particular. She lives in Gilroy now, works as a nurse, and claims the man's desertion was the best thing that ever happened to her. She can be a real bitch, especially to her second husband. He sometimes wonders if she's to blame for driving his father away.

Mid-afternoon sunlight ekes through the bar's single grubby porthole window, offending the gloom. The bartender evades the shaft of light and asks, "Meeting someone?" Shaun nods. "It's been a while since we've had a kid in here." The man points to his empty bottle and replaces it with a fresh one.

If the bastard doesn't show before he finishes, he'll go to Martuni's early, order a Cosmopolitan to clear his head and disinfect himself of this mistake. He'll confess to Brandon, make a joke of the incident. Describe the bar's decrepitude and decayed customers. Try to explain the surreal displacement he experienced, half-expecting a crowd of afterwork drinkers from SOMA's old machine shops to file inside.

His phone rings. The man informs him that he's running late (no shit!) but he's in the city now and parking in the garage at Mission Street. He hangs up before Shaun has a chance to reply. Rude fucker. He's tempted to give the man the finger by leaving, just as the bastard did to him and his mother twenty years ago. But hiking his ass out of here means that nothing will change. The man will continue to control his life by remote forever. Better to discover he has absolutely nothing in common with this tacky, gravel-voiced stranger. Consign him to spam. An old deposit that no longer accrues interest.

Clancy's door suddenly flies open, bringing with it a tsunami of litter from the sidewalk and the screeching brakes of a Muni bus. He turns as a figure appears, silhouetted against the light. Shaun blinks twice, trying to make out a phantom he yearns to recognize.

-end-

Beijing Poem: In Jintailu Station
Jennifer Fossenbell

a million pixels lit in two million eyes / this is
shine city / where all the people are / PLEIN in full bling
on the sleeve of a jacket / a clown's face embossed in gold
on the back / the glamor of passing through / canned station
music
in my head all night / the price we all pay / for moving
forward / this is a transfer station / I see no room to enter / then
the
pusher
with her uniform and shield shoves four men in at my back /
applies pressure
to the masses / and we are in / like a wall of bodies / in this land of
walls / it's not a wall
but a proliferation / bricks with faces / I think how every face is
distinct /
now I understand
how cereal settles / the train lurches / sudden velocity opens
space
between bodies
to be filled instantly by bodies sifting tighter / how no face is
real / or
all of us have the same face / the petite firefighter with pink
lipstick
the key is to dash into the car's inner chamber / another dimension
/ or get stuck
in the interdoor vortex / agitate at every stop like laundry

\\\ the ultrasound scan is called 4D \ the 4th dimension being
interiority

all of us have the same face / the mad cartoon pig on a swine flu
PSA / please
get ready for your arrival / it's astounding
how seldom you smell a fart / surrounded as we are in this
container
by so many bowels / traveling amid hundreds of armpits
and assholes / spleens, wrists and stomachs / nostrils and
eyebrows /
and not one of them
gives me their seat / my belly hidden in my coat / there's a
woman standing
in spike heels / how I ache looking at her / the press of creation
grows
less tolerable by the week / MEOW MEOW sequined on the
sleeve of a jacket
how very close
is communicability to commuting / we are
transmitted across the city / every
morning / crossing a dozen lines
some of them twice / I memorize characters
by sight and sound / none of the faces look the same
but they are all the same
face / look upon these divine tidings of comfort / green platform
soles /
a single padded seat

\\\ a face appears like a satellite image of a far planet \ and I guess
that
is him \ we read the surface for signs of life \ a familiar landform \ a
mouth \ a miracle \ a nose \ an alien feature inside me \ a face that
is
his face \ now he is a he \ I think he might be real \ after all \ if we
can
see him we might reach him \ might arrive at him one day

Beijing Poem: Donghuqu Station
Jennifer Fossenbell

2 months in & so sentimental already / not just the weep but the shudder-huff / the thing my dad does when overcome / listening to Simon & Garfunkel / I see his face from the past with the percussion from my lips / such a tiny sound / like the smallest hurting / like how much the soul can remember of god / wrapped in the starry womb & kicking in the dark / desperate to go through it / / no no, you are not yet sweet / you are an unripe fruit / lacking character almost / so far you have only a mass that is your own / a primal cellular intent to live / your minute need machine thrums near my liver / yet you are mine as much as my body is / or not at all / later you will make yourself visible after lunch / if anyone is watching / they spy a small fry flopping in my water-bag / make

there's a foreigner in my midst / B said how weird / to have not me inside of me / and it is / the most private invasion / by invitation / othering through intimacy / we are concentric peoples / my sweet amoebae

comments like future soccer player / already a little bruiser / or oh! you're positively glowing / listen / every one of us starts with a bruise / & I'm not glowing I'm flashing motherfuckrr / not even born my babe and already the world stacks narratives around us / we live inside their walls every day / in their balloons / I am *laowai* and *yunfu* on the metro / neither of us can be invisible anymore / a woman shoots a selfie with me in it behind her / I look straight at her screen / / *I see you* / I will be seen seeing being seen / after work on the platform small screens flicker in the corner of my eye / mimic an approaching train or a tear / a glint of this first utterly untranslatable fact / that we start encircled and end up encircling

The Ghost Lights
Ricardo José González-Rothi

There is smoke coming from the chimney of that house. said Angela, as she grappled with her blouse and sweater in the back seat of the car.

What house? Ajit seemed annoyed, struggling to zip his pants while crawling towards the drivers' seat.

The large house up the hill backed on to the north end of the park had seemed uninhabited for several years. The three-story building was now backlit by the moon. Indeed, smoke seemed to be floating from the main chimney. The house was completely dark inside. Ajit noticed there were no curtains in any of the windows.

Ain't nobody lived there in that big ole white monster for a couple of years… Ajit recalled one of the park caretakers saying he heard the house belonged to an old Indian couple who had either abandoned it or left it in their will to the park property.

But the smoke…Should we call the fire department? Angela began to fret.

Ajit started up the engine, backed out in darkness and drove towards the locked entry gate, leaving the park. He dropped Angela off as usual, about a block from her house. She lived in an exclusive gated community and preferred to walk the rest of the way. Her parents assumed the "Ajit" she spoke of was a high school girlfriend and Angela was good with that. They wouldn't have approved of him anyway.

The following Wednesday they were back at Riva and parked in their usual spot. The night was dark. It had been snowing and Ajit had pulled in beneath a tree towards the end of the parking lot. There were two or three inches of snow on the ground by now. They longed for these weekly dates, sneaking off to the park in Ajit's car after hours. Ajit had been a sports counselor at the park the prior summer and he had kept a key to the toll gate that usually closed the only entry after dark. The park was fairly extensive, with sport facilities, hiking trails and natural areas. They had the place to themselves. Ajit knew the place well enough that he could drive it in and out in the dark and access the gate without being seen.

They lowered the back seats of the SUV and unrolled a blanket. Angela seemed unusually fidgety that night. Ajit rolled his eyes as he struggled to undo his belt. Angela slipped off her coat, pulled up her skirt and straddled him. His hands roamed inside her blouse. Then Angela paused. She turned her head awkwardly towards the windshield, pushing his hands away from her breasts. *Wait...something is burning.* Ajit looked up, exasperated.

There is the damned smoke again... he said. *There has got to be someone inside that house.*

The once white house, a mammoth structure, with a covered hotel-like portico with columns over a circular driveway was now mildewed, and the paint was peeling off the painted brick around the sides and back. There were no screens on the windows, no garden chairs, potted plants or garden ornaments. For a house that might have cost well over a million dollars to build, the place was surprisingly absent of landscaping around it. The grass and surrounding area looked manicured, which is also why Ajit assumed perhaps the house was now property of the park, as he had seen the park mowers run the turf along the whole back end and sides.

Will it make you feel better if we have a look up close? Ajit took care to shut the car door quietly.

Angela followed him up the hill. They peeked through the sliding glass door to the lower floor at the back of the house. It was completely dark and the place looked empty. They walked around the side towards the garage. No outside lights, no cars in the driveway. No footprints in the snow leading to or from the front door. No apparent sounds coming from the house. Ajit used the flashlight on his cell phone. The moisture in his exhaled breath condensed like a tiny ice cloud around him.

Electric meter doesn't look like it is running. Gas line must also be shut off. Pipe is disconnected.

They could smell a fragrant smell of the smoke from the

chimney. It reminded Ajit of incense. Surprisingly there were no stacks of firewood outside anywhere. They walked back down the hill and into Ajit's car, both got in through the same back door of his SUV.

Now, where were we? Angela pulled Ajit towards him, leaning back. He climbed onto her.

His jet blue-black hair draped over Angela's red curls made for an eerie contrast in the moonlight. Ajit knew his Maa would not approve. His mother's influence on him started back in the womb, deep roots sutured into his consciousness trumping his anticipation with a hint of guilt. After all, she was his *Janani*, the mother who gave him birth. But the guilt would be fleeting. He grunted with lust as his hands maneuvered inside Angela's unbuttoned jeans.

The following day, a bright but cold Saturday morning, Ajit felt compelled to drive back to the park early. *What if someone lived in that house and caught them in the act?* He imagined the cops coming, and both he and Angela taken to the police station and charged with "minors fornicating on public property". He pictured the headlines.

That morning there were no cars or people around. Ajit walked up the paved path towards the ball fields, about one hundred yards at the bottom of the hill behind where the white house stood. Leaning over a field fence, he pulled out binoculars, and scanned each window and door carefully for signs of any movement. Nothing. He then ambled into the thick woods north of where the house was, careful not to be noticed. He strapped a game camera onto a tree trunk in a discreet location, aiming it so that it would cover for any motion along the back and one side of the house at the level of the windows and back doors on the main floor living area. After double-checking the settings for video and infrared recording, he left.

That night Ajit dreamt that he was inside a cave and Bagalamukhi, the goddess who paralyzes enemies, knees on either side of his hips, was straddling him. She looked down at his face. He felt the energy of her gleaming eyes burning through his chest and then he began to have trouble breathing. The smell of sandalwood smoke in the cave overpowered him. Looking past Bagalamuki's shoulder towards the cave ceiling, he saw a young woman with pale skin and wavy red hair in the background. She maneuvered behind Bagalamukhi, arms trying to reach around the goddess in desperate attempts to grasp for him. But the goddess held her back. Ajit remembered his mother telling him when he was little that Bagalamukhi would always keep him safe, as long as he called on the *Mantra Shakti* to help and guide him. There was a shattering, high-pitch sound, like glass breaking and then what sounded like a woman's muffled scream. Ajit was now fully awake, or so he thought. Bagalamukhi was gone but the red-haired woman now knelt beside him, hands cupping her naked breasts close to his face. The woman's face was grossly distorted, and thick clumps of her curls began to shed off her scalp onto Ajit's face. He awoke in a sweat, unable to go back to sleep.

Over the next several days, Ajit became obsessed with the house up the hill. He would drive to the park at random hours, methodically scanning the house for any signs of occupancy. He checked the trash container regularly, and it was always empty.

One evening, he waited until the park was about to close, and meandered into the wooded area by the house. He reached the game camera and retrieved the sim card. Later, he screened through 108 instances where the camera was triggered and video had been recorded. There were no images whatsoever during daylight hours despite the shutter being triggered. However, in darkness, the infrared videos showed images of what appeared to be a soft glow of light, like that of a flickering candle against inside walls. The pulsing light was captured through different windows, in no particular sequence, and several instances in the large room which opened onto a sliding door on the back of the house. In several images, what looked like a cast shadow could be seen near the central staircase but Ajit was unable to identify whether it was that of a human figure or just light artifact. One last image, timed at 5:47am that early morning, before sunrise, showed movement in an unexpected area. The infrared clearly revealed an opening and then closing of an oddly placed door near the rear corner on the outside wall.

The door was oddly placed because it opened out to the outside second story of the house but there was no balcony and no railing. Ajit was perplexed. He counted the number of captured events again: One hundred and eight. Exactly fifty-four during daylight hours and 54 in the dark. Was this just coincidence?

That night, Ajit fingered his *mala* beads and began to repeat his mantra, as his Maa had taught him since he was old enough to remember. One hundred and eight-that is how many *rudraksha* seeds were in the Hindu prayer garland! The sacred number. One hundred and eight lines of energy from your heart chakra, 108 stages of the journey of the human soul of Hindus. Even the Buddhist prayer beads had 108 virtues to cultivate in order to balance a possible 108 "defilements". He would not tell Angela about the video images. He also would not tell her about the dream. Benevolent as Bagalamukhi could be, Ajit knew she was also capable of blocking the life force in living beings and cause death.

Ajit was at a crossroads. He was tired of striving to be "the good son." He was tired of hiding the lust for his *gora* girlfriend. It was as if all the karma stuff and gurus and mantras that had been so ingrained in him by his Maa, his *Janani*, were now smothering him. He saw himself slipping down a path of godlessness instead of godliness.

Unable to sleep, Ajit awoke while it was still dark and slid out of the house taking care not to wake his parents. He made up his mind to go to Riva park one last time. There were residual snow patches on the ground. Climbing up the hill to the house he slipped in the muddy turf several times before reaching the front door, inadvertently rubbing his face with a muddy glove, which made him look like a madman. No one was around. He went up the entry steps and pressed the doorbell repeatedly. No reply. He knocked loudly,

"Anybody home? Hello? Hello?" He pounded with a closed fist several more times. "Open this fukking door, you *Jhaantu*! Do you hear me? Open this door!" he shouted. Still no answer.

Resolved to put the whole issue of the house and the smoke and the glowing lights behind him, Ajit went down the front door steps and around towards the back of the house and started down the hill, towards his car. It was almost daylight by now. A few steps away from the back corner of the house, he heard a sound behind and above him. He turned. The "odd door" opening onto nowhere on the second floor was open. He could see the figure of an old woman dressed in a yellow sari standing on the edge. She looked towards him and smiling, extended her arm outwards, opening her hand. She dropped what looked like several bread crumbs off into the air. Before the morsels hit the ground, and as if out of nowhere, several crows appeared, catching all of the pieces mid-air. All but one. The birds flew off, startled, when out of the single breadcrumb on the ground unfurled a serpentine figure. It was a cobra! The reptile slithered slowly off the patch of snow where the crumb had landed. It then coiled and raised its head, waving it rhythmically side-to-side as if in a trance. The woman in the yellow sari smiled and shut the door.

Father Asks Me to Consider the Path of Mme. Lebrun, Royal Portraitist

Jana Harris

Rue de la Bienfaisance, Paris, 1838

(Rosa Bonheur, b. 1822)

I just wanted to draw horses.

Baroque portraits, Biblical motifs,
peasant scenes, seascapes;
at the Louvre I made endless studies:
the Bruegels, Rembrandt, Raphael. First
I sold one copy--a hundred francs,
one month's wages for a laborer--
then another, lining Father's pockets.
Seek your way, Rosa. Surpass Mme. Lebrun,
Pere instructed over and over.
In her 80's, just having published
a memoir in three volumes,
Elisabeth Vigee-Lebrun's disclosures
were on everyone's lips.

Her name rattled inside my head;
I saw double. Like me, her father an artist,
her childhood filled with painters.
At eleven she could manage a palette;
at thirteen, invited to study noble collections;
at fourteen she copied the works of Rubens.
At my age she already painted professionally
and exhibited at the annual Salon.

Her father died. She married

an art dealer who drank and gambled.
At seventeen she supported her mother
and brother and husband.
She acquired charm—
something to think about.

Mme. Lebrun always painted from life,
let that be a lesson to me.
To support her growing family
she took on students
and in her Souvenirs confessed
that incessantly touching-up their work
irritated her sharply.

In her twenties she became portraitist
to the Queen; at twenty-eight elected
to the French Royal Academy—
despite rumors that she'd painted
Marie Antoinette in her night dress
and the King's finance minister without legs
so that he could not run away from her.

Exiled to Italy, Austria, Russia;
she painted the children of monarchs.
Nearly six-hundred portraits!
Here Pere's voice climbed an octave;
a member of many Fine Arts Academies.
He counted triumphs, tongue tripping,
eyes filling first with awe then ire.

How many, I wondered, of the hundreds
were self-portraits? Why
she so often painted
her comely smiling self, sometimes
with her daughter, echoing
a Rubens Madonna and child?
Why was she always looking in a mirror?

Filling a need, Pere replied,
to address painterly problems.

Could he not see it would be madness
for me to follow this path?

I just wanted to draw horses.

Recipe for Viewing the Perseids
Sarath Reddy

It's not enough to pray for cloudless nights
moon carved into crescent, sparkling stage
beyond distracting city bling. Seek out
untamed countryside or shore embracing sea.
Your naked eyes acquainted with the dark
await midnight when the show begins,
no telescope to draw the drama near.
Welcome celestial music inside--
adagio, sonata, your own aria.
Remember the last time you were in love,
that burn within for someone far away?
As your song swells, sway gently, tune your gaze
and search slowly each swathe of crowded sky
for comet tails that jet between the stars.

The Sound Frequencies Made by Spider Silk

Alice B Fogel

Stand still in the woods to silence
    the sliding of small stones and time-slimmed leaves
and if for a moment there is no breeze to shuffle
    branches and no jet slices overhead and no saw
or compressor runs in the distance and no stream sluices
    over rocks and not a single deer pulls up grass, no mice
or voles slink under the decay and scruff of the forest,
    and if no shale shifts or scree slips down a slope, then

if you listen you might hear the tappings of the spider's
    sensors on a strand of her web—limbs of her own body—
and the signal it sends. How long, how far, how framed
    and spiraled: these compose the frequencies, the tones
and rhythms bound to how dry the duff of the ground,
    how thick and sticky the plucked silk, how far and reaching
and tightly strung its every vibration over air, to shape
    this ring of anchor, of capture, this hum of hub and scrape.

And if the heat rising doesn't make the male peak and die
    before his time comes to copulate, or before she—tied
instead to degrees of light radiating through the global orb—
    is primed to reproduce, and if the web doesn't fail to sing
with insects diminishing from pesticides and single crops
    starving the soil, then each finely tuned stretch of thread
will be a zephyr shivering sound waves to play her lures,
    to spin in spokes, to make a music of her meal and mate.

Heat Flood
Arshia Batra

The last ice cap melted. The last fish shriveled.
A cloud of our water condenses around us, hugs
Skin as if to plead acknowledgment. Now, do
You see? Almighty angels, untouchable, their
Presence suffocating. They cannot heal, only
Ring halos like hopeless infinities. When all
Of humanity lays down weapon, simply because
It is too hard to breathe. Lays down everything in its
Hands—food, money, children. Lays down bodies.
The sun bulges like an unclosing eye, a breast
Overflowing with the shine we once suckled so
Carelessly. Now, do you see? The planet's arteries,
Empty. Batting rays furiously: Now, do you see?
But it was too hot.

Such a Small Thing
Pam McFarland

Rick Bellaman couldn't stand the thought of being away from Gertie, Justin, and Samantha, for one second longer. He had gone in to the office only because the university required him to keep an eye on what was happening. The thing, a bright, comet-like object the scientific community first had mistaken for a distant planet or star, then, in disbelief, saw it for what it was: an asteroid, hurtling straight toward Earth. Then they all thought that it would safely pass by the planet. But the calculations had changed. How could something so lovely, so exquisitely formed, be so lethal? Efforts to shoot down the asteroid with missiles had failed. They were all quite simply: screwed. The asteroid, expected to make contact within the next twenty hours, would likely create a dust cloud so enormous that most people—possibly all people—would die.

He knew Gertie was already waiting, for him at home. They had decided they wouldn't tell the children. She had come up with the stroke-of-genius idea of a family summer camp, which delighted Justin at least. And it gave Gertie something to do other than wring her hands. He helped her set up two pup tents in the living room, one for Justin, one for Samantha, next to a larger tent for Gertie and him. No news, no phones, no television. Samantha had wanted to know why she couldn't have her phone, contact her friends, most of whom to her knowledge were attending real summer camps, although Rick suspected that most of their parents had imposed equally protective measures in their homes. Around midweek, though, the novelty had worn off, and they abandoned the tents, returning to their rooms.

How do you prepare a child for something like this? It agonized him to think what they might already know. Samantha, ten, probably had figured something out, somehow, despite Gertie's best efforts. She was trying too hard to appear normal, like how she had pretended to believe in Santa Claus well past the time she didn't, in that strange and tender way children feel they must protect their parents from knowing the painful truth they are growing up.

Terrified people, desperate to get somewhere, jammed the road. Rick shook his head. Nothing mattered at this point. Nowhere to go. Visible heat waves simmered up from the asphalt. The air conditioner was busted, but he wouldn't roll down the window to let in the sounds of humanity all around him. He could hear horns, people shouting, helicopters flying around as if someone in charge could corral everything into some semblance of order. There was nothing anyone could do. He set his phone to his Billie Holiday list and plugged it into the USB port.

He noticed two drivers—their cars pinned together in an apparent fender bender—on the road's shoulder. They were shouting into each other's faces. One raised his fists as if he planned to hit the other driver, punctuating whatever he was saying with an angry index finger. What a waste of time and energy. He drove by and promptly forgot them.

* * *

Janie Wilkins paced in her apartment. She looked out the window. Beautiful blue sky. Hot. She didn't know whom to call. This experiment of moving from St. Louis to D.C. after her parents died had utterly failed. She had no one. She pulled out her Bible and tried to read, but her eyes couldn't focus, and she rocked back and forth on the chair, reciting what she remembered of the Lord's Prayer. She kept messing the words up. She so wished there was someone she could talk to. She had thought about calling the church to talk to the pastor about Heaven and Hell privately. But she had been too timid about asking such a question, and now it was too late to even try to get to a service she had seen advertised online.

* * *

At the altar, Roberta Peabody's hand shook as she lit the thick cylindrical candle. Red, for Pentecost, the time when the people first began speaking in tongues and different languages, on fire with the breath of the Lord. She had always thought people focused too much on the wrong part of the story. What truly mattered, in her mind at least, was the fact that the universal language of God, pure love, required no words at all. She straightened her spine and turned around, smiling at the twenty or thirty people who had gathered. So many of them she knew so intimately, she felt a sort of love toward them. She had borne witness to their joys, their trials, and sorrows for more than twenty years, some of them. She would not let them see her fear now, even though her legs felt like they would collapse. She looked at the congregants who stared back at her, wanting reassurance from her that everything would be all right somehow. She rubbed her damp palms on her robes and cleared her throat. "Let us stand," she said.

* * *

Cat Olson wanted to get to the church shelter to get cleaned up but didn't think they'd let her in. All the churches in town seemed to be busy. She hadn't had a shower for days, and her clothes reeked. She just wanted to find someplace quiet, away from the crazy chaos that had seized the city. She had seen an older man in a business suit muttering incoherently directly in front of her, wandering in a sort of daze. His eyes had been frantic, terrified, and they looked right through her, like she wasn't even there. Perhaps she really had become invisible. She couldn't remember the specifics of how she ended up here on the street, other than she had. She had always had trouble managing things that seemed easy for other people, like understanding when someone was angry or, conversely, happy to see her. She could not read faces. She had lived in shelter for a while, but after her bags had been stolen for the second or third time, she decided to live out here, on the street. She felt safer.

* * *

Janie had called her therapist five times in the past three hours. All she got was voicemail. Her therapist had abandoned her. It's not like she called her often. The one time she needed her, the woman didn't return her calls or texts. She peered down at her phone again, willing the little dots to appear, or a message. Something. Nothing at all.

* * *

The clusterfuck around the university campus had cleared, and Rick navigated the traffic down the back roads toward home, noticing how intensely green trees the trees were. They had come into full bloom in the past few weeks. He drove past the state park where he had gone swimming as a teenager, where he had had his first kiss, with Melanie Carrols. He could see it in his mind, even with his eyes focused on the road. There they were, standing face to face in the middle of the creek, on the slippery stones poking out of the shallow water, with the warm sun on their backs. She smiled at him. His body trembling, he leaned forward and brushed her lips with his. They were both sixteen.

Rick suddenly couldn't see anything, and he brought his knuckle to his mouth to stop the sob that caught in his throat.

* * *

Roberta yanked out the plate with the plastic cups and the loaf of bread. Who was going to stop her now? It was everyone for themselves at this point. The senior minister had gone to his place at the Shore with his family, and the others, who knew they where had crawled off to. She had pleaded with Jason to hold the church open for anyone who wandered in, as a comfort. He had agreed, reluctantly even though she was no longer on staff at the church. She was only a lay leader. She had been stripped of her ordination after people found out about her relationship with, Kathleen, for two years after her divorce. No matter that it had eventually ended, much to her sorrow, and that she had been married to Charlie prior to that for fifteen years, thirteen of those happily, whole-heartedly. But she wouldn't let her mind go down that path. Not now. She had to focus.

She poured the grape juice into the tiny cups, picturing the lily-livered bishop's face as he had told her. He had looked sad, sympathetic, but not enough to stand up for her. He wasn't going to risk losing his own job over her. Fuck that. She was going to pray for the blessing of the holy cup and allow anyone who wanted and needed ablution to be able to have it, not the least of all herself, and damn anyone to tell her not to.

* * *

Rick drove over the wooden planks of the bridge near his house and avoided looking toward the mature willows on both sides, which he knew were prettily draping their lower branches over the faded railings. Gertie loved those trees. She loved nature period, the colorful pop of one or two wild roses in a sea of brush and weeds that she would capture in the photos they put up all over their house. She could catch the smallest, most miniscule details, things he'd never even notice. He rubbed his eyes. She hadn't answered when he called earlier. She was probably tied up making sure Samantha and Justin were okay. Maybe she had succeeded in getting them interested in camping in the living room again. He drove past the field where he threw a baseball back and forth with Justin after dinner most nights, even just a few weeks ago, when everything was still normal, then pulled into the driveway. Home.

She was there in the doorway when he walked up. She pulled the door open, and he wrapped his arms around her thin body and held her. "You okay?" he asked. She nodded, though he could see her eyes were wet. "How about the kids?" he whispered.

Gertie put her hands on both sides of his face before kissing him. "They are doing about as well as any of us are. I don't know if Samantha knows or not. But we're here. We're all together. I'm glad you got home."

"I called you," he said.

"I've been trying not to look at the phone," she said.

Rick picked her phone, which was sitting on the kitchen counter up. "You've got a bunch of messages from a 202 number."

She shook her head. "It's one of my clients. I can't focus on anything now but us. I've made a nice dinner. We'll eat. And we can try to enjoy it." No reference to the asteroid. It didn't surprise him. Gertie had always been down-to-Earth, pragmatic, willing to face any challenge or crisis head on. Maybe that was a better approach, rather than agonizing over everything that was loved and soon lost.

Rick scrolled through the list of texts and calls. "I know you're not supposed to talk about your clients with me, but this person has left you a lot of messages."

Gertie snatched the phone. "Give me that." She looked at the messages, then met his gaze. "Like I said, I'm not focusing on my clients right now. I can't."

"Yeah, but if this person is in crisis, maybe a word from you could help them."

"Everybody is in crisis right now. Nothing I say is going to make a difference. And stop trying to look at my phone. This is all confidential information."

"What's it going to cost you?"

"A few minutes of what's left of my precious life," she said, her voice rising.

"Shh. Okay." He pulled her toward him again. "Don't call them. It's too late, anyway."

Gertie was stiff in his arms. She frowned, her eyes fierce. "Damn it, Rick. All right, I will call this person back."

* * *

Janie jumped when she heard the cell phone. She wasn't expecting anyone to call her at this point.

"Hello, Janie, how are you doing?"

Janie wanted to weep at hearing the comfortable familiarity, the sheer normalcy, of Gertie's voice.

"Not so good," Janie's voice warbled.

"What would help you right now?"

"I'm just so scared."

"Honey, I think we all are. There's nothing I can say that can make things better for you. I'm not going to lie to you. But I believe that you're a good person. Most of us doing our best, and in the end, maybe that's what matters. Is there something you could do, or someone you could call to talk to over the next couple of hours?"

"I wanted to go to church," Janie said. She was surprised at how calm her voice sounded.

"Well, why can't you?"

"It's too late. The service was a few hours ago."

"Well, is there someone you could call from church?"

Janie thought of the people she knew at church. She tended to show up and leave immediately when the service ended. But she did know one of the adult Sunday School teachers, sort of. After she ended the call with Gertie, she searched in the church directory for the phone number of the woman, Colleen, who was about her age.

She had been surprised when Colleen picked up, seemed glad to hear from her, had told her that the church was open to anyone who wanted to come. Just to be with other people would be a comfort. She picked up a green short-sleeved dress that had been draped over the arm of a chair. She wriggled into the soft fabric, appreciating the way it felt on her skin, and admired how pretty she looked in the mirror. She loved the yellow roses that spilled across the top layer of chiffon fabric. She was twenty-three. She thought about Todd, the guy she had just started to date. She had kind of liked him. He was a good kisser, and he made her laugh. She thought maybe he liked her too, but he had disappeared since the news came out about the asteroid. But then why wouldn't he? Things hadn't gotten serious between them yet. But she wished. She wished she could have experienced love. Love in the Grand sense, not the small. But she wasn't going to think about that now. She wanted to be in a churchto take communion, so she could be forgiven for any sins she had committed. She walked down the street to catch a bus headed downtown. She felt less terrified, more curious. What would happen to them all?

* * *

Cat looked at the jittery young woman who sat beside her at the bus stop where she often slept. She was surprised that the woman – she couldn't be more than twenty or twenty-one, had seated herself on the bench directly next to her. Not that there was a whole lot of room, but most people kept their distance. Maybe the girl hadn't noticed Cat's fallen state. Fallen in the sense of dropping completely out of the world to an entirely different place, not in the sense of being fallen in the eyes of God.

Cat tried to talk with her. She did like to have conversations with people she encountered at the bus stop. But after about a minute, Cat shut her mouth. Because the woman got that expression in her eyes, the same one that people always got eventually after listening to her speak, that told her she'd said too much of the wrong thing. This woman, though, didn't step away, or purposefully avoid looking at her. And when Cat asked for money to get a cup of coffee, the woman took a dollar bill out of her tidy little purse and pressed it into Cat's palm, looking her right in the eyes. After the bus came and went, Cat thought about the way the woman – really, still a girl – had looked, in her cool-looking green dress with yellow flowers. She had been so kind, with not an ounce of pity or overwrought piety. Somehow, the young woman had seen her.

* * *

Roberta walked down the aisle, collecting the communion plates with the now-empty cups. She would never be able to understand why people tended to see things in such black and white terms, failing to acknowledge the beautiful and complicated nuances of life. Well, that was changing. The younger generations could care less about so many things that derailed entire careers, lifetimes in the older generations. Maybe many things might have changed. But not in this way. Not with everything ending like this before humanity had figured things out, somehow finding a way to live without destroying itself. How could a loving God allow this to happen? It went against everything she had always believed.

Her eyes filled with tears. The congregants. The elderly Greeleys. Bev McGruder and her twin girls, who were struggling after their father had died of cancer. Dick and Lacey Johnson. These were her people. She reached the altar and placed the plates in a pile on top, then leaned on it, her breath growing ragged.

The organist, Al, who was an institution and been there for many more years than she had— and that was saying something—got up from his perch behind the organ and put his arm around her back.

"You, okay?"

She leaned into him. "Yes, of course. Give me a minute. And then could you play a few hymns? We can all sing along."

"You got it sweetheart," he said. He squeezed her shoulders in a quick hug and rubbed her back with the back of his palm in a reassuring circle. Such a small thing, but it made her feel better. Roberta watched him return to the organ before she turned to face the congregation. It dawned on her that what the church officials formally decreed didn't matter. She was here, doing what she loved. No one could stop her from tending to others. "Let us stand and turn to 'Amazing Grace' on page 378 of your hymnals." When she opened her mouth to sing, she found the words she thought she would never be able to believe again at the tip of her tongue, and her heart filled, inexplicably, with a kind of joy.

* * *

Dinner had been had, and they had gotten through it. Every word, every gesture seemed to carry import. They had eaten out on the screened-in porch and talked about ordinary things while listening to peep frogs and other night sounds. They watched a doe and her two fawns cross the lawn, chewing on the grass and watching them, eyes alert, and Justin pointed to the bats flitting around the oak trees at the back of the yard. Justin loved the bats.

After the kids went inside to get ready for bed, he and Gertie had both had a glass of wine and lingered until it was almost too dark to see anything beyond the citronella lighting the table. They went in to say goodnight. Gertie crawled into bed with Justin and read to him from the early reader chapter book they had begun reading together. She curled her finger around the stray lock of hair that fell into his eyes most of the time, then kissed him on the forehead. They paused at Samantha's door. Rick and she both stood, taking in her loveliness before she snuggled under the covers to read. "No more than half an hour," Rick said.

Alone together in the hallway, Gertie turned to face him." I'm going to take an Ativan, then am going to bed. Don't wait too long."

"I'll be in in just a minute."

He went into the den and angled the telescope toward the sky. There it was. Luminous. Beautiful. With no will of its own. The papers, media, various overly religious types, had gotten it all wrong, characterizing it as some sort of divine retribution, or a sort of malevolent force sent to bring about Armageddon. That asteroid carried no malice. It was not a sentient being. The Earth just happened to be in the way. That was all. He didn't know if he believed in a God or not. But he hoped there was a God, of some sort, and that he, and Gertie, and his family would go on somehow. He couldn't bear to think that they wouldn't. But it was what it was, whatever *it* happened to be. He glanced once more at the night-time sky, then turned the telescope lens to face the wall.

Gertie was already knocked out. The wine from dinner plus the Ativan had done what they needed to. For a moment, he wanted to shake her awake, so they could lay each other's arms for a few minutes more and talk for as long as they could, maybe have sex. But he decided to let her sleep. Rick leaned over his wife, inhaled her familiar honeysuckle talcum powder scent, and kissed the cool solid nape of her neck. He turned off the light on the headboard and leaned back. But he sat back up. He couldn't sleep. He turned and faced his wife, watching her slow, even breaths go in and out, in and out. He had never seen anything so beautiful, except maybe the scrunched-up and furious faces of Justin and Samantha when they first came into the world.

After a time, he decided he would get up. He quietly got out of bed, careful not to wake Gertie. He padded into the den and positioned the telescope to face the dark night sky, sat in the comfortable chair by the window, and waited.

What To Do While Waiting For The Poem
J.R. Solonche

While waiting for the poem,
you should write a poem.
Not the one you are waiting for,
which will be the great poem,
the perfect, shining poem
that rises resplendent in the east
of your mind like an Aegean sunrise.
Not that one which will be
the flawless diamond of a poem,
the hardest of all you shall ever write,
against which all others are tested.
The poem you write while waiting
for that poem, will be a tear-shaped
piece of glass to trick the heart.

The Empty Seat

He plays religiously to a full house. At a black grand piano at the center of an otherwise barren stage. He performs regardless of the weather or the time of year or the whims of the economy and the rigors of our existence. A single performance, every third month, always on the last day of the month. Be it a Saturday or a Monday or any other day. Irrespective of competing forms of entertainment. He played opposite the Final Four twice, and he performed one year to the accompaniment of the ominous winds of a slowly approaching hurricane. Even then it seemed every seat was taken. He played one Easter Sunday. One Good Friday. And, of course, he plays every New Year's Eve.

In spite of the occasion, he never varies his selections. Like the regularity of his appearances, they are a reliable constant in our lives, executed in identical order each and every time. There is not so much as the slightest deviation in the length of the intervals between the pieces or in the extent of his brief intermissions.

And his musicality is also forever the same—soft and clean and precise with complex rhythms that are extended just as far as they can be without dissolving themselves into disorder or dishonor. Final notes sustained until not even he can discern them. Whether they be his own creations or his unique arrangements of the familiar works of others. He plays with meticulous fingers both the piano and the slack-key guitar with an occasional diversion on the harmonica or flute. He plays to us and for us, although he is not one of us. We are a small yet bustling Southern town holding on tightly to our traditions and our cherished beliefs. Not that we aren't ceding them slowly, methodically to the ineluctable wave of progress.

Yet we have saved our old town hall building and the venerable theater nested within where he performs. Scrupulously maintained the mid-nineteenth-century, hybrid-neoclassical/Victorian design and detail—down to the elaborately brocaded red chairs, flanking tiers of box seats with their rich, velvety curtains, and small, steep-pitched balcony with its creaky, oaken floor. Even the antique crystal chandelier hanging above and the ornate, gilded detailing in the Corinthian columns and intricate woodwork all around. We preserve these things for ourselves and our children and hopefully their children and beyond. To keep culture and our honored past alive as long as we possibly can.

He has nothing to do with that past. And we really do not know him. Rumor is he was from the West originally, and indeed his music is reminiscent of the vast and empty stretches there. Of the openness and the endlessness. And yet his music subsumes a host of influences—jazz, blues, folk, popular, rock, classical, and swing. Even Hawaiian and a hint of Oriental. He must have traveled widely to study euphony and its evolution. And so he is in a sense not of any one place or of any one time. Yet despite his travels and his many interests, he always returns to us trimonthly on the final day, concluding each and every piece with the same simple refrain to our appreciative applause: "Thank you. You are so kind. Much too kind."

I don't know who first noticed. Or for that matter the particular performance. But I do remember the shock of the realization, the simultaneous absurdity and undeniable truthfulness of it. And how quickly the reality spread among us. First the older folks, then those of my generation, finally the children from whom we tried to hide the revelation. Foolishly believing that the knowledge would frighten them away from the theater. And perhaps from us. Thinking that they would lose faith in their parents and their traditions, in the hallowed music hall and the reveries inspired by our periodic visitor.

"Reverie" doesn't capture the state his harmonies induce in us. But I'm not sure there is a word for it or ever will be. For the charm of it and the feeling of being lost for a spell. At times, it feels as if I were floating alone and unimpeded upon the surface of a fathomless, lifeless sea, supine to a night sky adorned always with the same nameless constellations, my naked body drifting in place to the immutable turn of the heavens. It is like sleeping a sleep with no dreams. As if life and all its concerns haven't so much been suspended for a moment as having never existed at all.

It isn't openly discussed in such terms of course. We all simply acknowledge that we love his music as much for the tradition of our gatherings as for its effect. And for the sense of being one in something. Huddled in the cozy theater all focused on his slight and fragile form, listening to the same rhythms according to the same cycle. Every third month, the last day of the month. Twenty-four fixed selections performed in an unassailable order. Each one concluded with the identically cadenced, "Thank you. You are so kind. Much too kind." Precisely 581 seats, perhaps a tenth of the town, slightly different points of view—from balcony to box seat, from orchestra to center to aisle—all converging on a vintage grand piano and the man who is both its master and ours for some two-odd hours, faithfully four times a year.

It was not this collective reverie that was one day noticed. We all knew of that from his very first appearance. Although it's an unspoken truth, even the children were immediately aware. Nor was it the strange fact that the house was always full. That not a single place was empty at the start of any of the multitude of his concerts over the years. We were, of course, amazed by this and wondered if there would come a time when every seat wasn't taken. An anxiety of sorts soon began to mount performance to performance, a kind of dread of the inevitable day the string would finally end. But years of accumulated apprehension dissolved completely the evening of the record snowfall. If nineteen inches of ice and snow, of hazardous roads and precarious walkways, of frigid temperatures and numbing winds—if all these factors couldn't create an empty seat, then nothing could.

Yet that *was* what was noticed. A seat unclaimed. Not at the beginning of any performance of course. But at the end. Always at the end, one single vacant spot. That is the word that one day quickly spread among us.

"There's always one empty seat at the conclusion of the

program."

"It was next to me this time."

"It moves about the hall. It is never in the same place. It was in the balcony this month. Last time it was at the very back. Once it was on the front row. But always there is an open seat."

"It's strange. The hall is always full at the beginning. And I have never seen a soul leave and not return."

"Who do you think it is? And how are they getting out?"

We soon eliminated the theory that someone was leaving early on each occasion, somehow unnoticed. Because we all diligently checked to our left and our right, in front and behind, to this diagonal and that to familiarize ourselves with our circle before each event. But come the end of the show when we had emerged from our rapture and a seat adjacent was unoccupied, none of us could recall just who had resided there.

"I know that place was taken."

"Yes, I can confirm it."

"Someone was there."

Yet no one can ever put their finger on exactly whom. At first, all surveyed their surroundings to confirm that each and every chair was occupied after intermission. For a time, guards were stationed outside the exit doors and in the front and rear of the theater to ensure that no one left the building. Or attempted to furtively sequester themselves in a back corner off the lobby or in the coat closet or a bathroom or behind the stage. And no one ever has. Unless you include those rare occasions when a member of the audience, suddenly taken ill or called out to an emergency, is forced to depart prematurely. But then someone else immediately takes their place. So popular are the performances, so much a staple of our lives, that there are always those waiting outside, in rain or cold, right up to the final number, for just such an opportunity. But even when the usual routine is interrupted by such substitutions, there is still a vacancy at the very end. Always a single, inexplicable abandoned chair.

I remember the moment the thought occurred to me. It was like a novel melody suddenly running through my mind. One that

I'd never heard before, but which had a strange familiarity to it, as if the notes had somehow always been resident within. Yes, the truth came suddenly, yet as undeniably as the age-old rhythms of the sun and stars: one of us is in fact disappearing. And it is our revered performer's music that somehow transports them away. Simultaneously erases not only every tangible evidence but the very memory of their existence. With the single exception, of course, of the void left by their absence—the stark reminder of that empty seat.

And that is why we all come back. That is why we cannot resist the ritual of his quarterly and altogether predictable reprise. But it isn't a sinister or lurid thrill that draws us in. Not some twisted desire to push the fates, to play roulette with our lives. Such are far from the emotion that fills us and the theater. Nor is it a death wish. I have no longing to perish or to lose the memory of any of my loved ones or my friends. And besides, none of that reconciles with the children: children aren't capable of such perverse desires. Nor are they in secret dread of the place, as we all had once feared. Although they know full well, as each of the adults, the reality of the empty seat.

And yet among us, just as in the mesmerizing effects of the music, none of this is directly spoken. Certainly the phenomenon of disappearance is acknowledged and in the open to all. But the reasons for it and the feelings about it are not the subject of communion, either between neighbors across the friendly backyard fence or among kith and kin within the cloistered walls of home. We each keep our thoughts to ourselves and assume that everyone shares a common view of the thing. That it is exceptional, even sublime, and that we are blessed in our otherwise ordinary, little Southern town with a glimpse to something beyond. And if we are one day indeed the one to be elided, then it is in the natural order of things.

I never look at it as a death. How can death exist without a memory of it? And I never consider asking *him*. Whether he knows what we know. All he ever confides to us is that he loves our theater and our loyalty. And that music is best when played to small audiences. In intimate settings before entire families.

Just as he faithfully reminds us prior to each recital that song is an art of purposeful repetition. He slips into town the afternoon of each appearance, spends the night in the same hotel in the very same room, and is out on the first flight the next morning. He is such a private man, and we feel so special to have him return with such frequency that we never dare to invade his solitude or to be so presumptuous as to pose to him just why he comes back again and again.

I do wonder, however, just where in his act our citizens disappear. Exactly what combination of chords and beat and tempo invoke the magic. There are times I feel as if I myself am about to be the chosen one. Instances when the trance-like state keeps building and building and I'm farther and farther away from all the others with each new subtlety. I wonder if it's a gradual process mounting from piece to piece or rather something that could transpire within any single selection. Whether the phenomenon is the same for all of us. Or perhaps for each unique. Somehow tuned precisely to our own particular rhythms and the singular melodies of our souls. But I never let my speculations spoil a show. Never allow them to interfere with the very same rapture and awe that I felt in those days before I realized what was occurring.

Ten years have passed since his first appearance, and now we find ourselves gathered together on yet another New Year's Eve. The empty seat has been within my reach four times. By evening's end some forty-one townsfolk will have occupied it. How many did I know well? How many were a friend or a neighbor? I never knew my father. But I know I must have had one. All that my mother ever said was that he disappeared long before I was born. But perhaps the truth is he was there for us all along, a loyal husband and devoted parent, passing away just this last year, each single memory and every shred of physical proof forever removed by the empty seat. I have a lovely wife and two daughters now. I question on occasion if there was a previous wife. Perhaps another child. The son I will never remember.

But none of that matters for the moment. The next performance is about to begin. And I am ready. As all of us are ready. In my mind even now, I can hear the full complement of his fixed repertoire in its perpetual order. Feel the imminent rhapsody and the ethereal distance and the numbing beauty. And as usual I carefully twist my program about itself once, twice, shift my weight to the right, cup my head in my hand, and focus my attention on the stage at the very instant he will walk out to take his seat to our opening applause.

Yes, I am ready should it be my turn. Certain that if it is, there will be no trace of me left behind.

Lot's Daughter
Kristin Zimet

Forward, he said, slapping my bottom like a donkey's rump.
At least I got a couple steps ahead of my sister's snuffling.
We left my stupid mother seized stiff as a rock. Never look
back, the messengers hammered my father, and if that is
the way a god behaves, bet your life you'd better do it, too.

A packet of dried dates, rags in case I bled, a waterskin,
no more than that. But no catcalls, no pinches, nobody left
to feel us up at market. Not a bad deal. What I brought out
was me, my breasts beginning to go round and bounce
and only one man now to reckon with. So I thought,

what if a new city starts in my belly, where I make the rules,
guzzle wine, and knock the men around? What if I choose
a man, ride him as I saw my father ride: slaves, my mother,
pretty boys who sell themselves for bread? And what if
I take him helpless, pay him back for slipping in beside me,

rubbing at me, all those nights I held my breath, afraid,
wondering, me or my little sister this time? Serve him right
for offering us to a mob like tossing meat to dogs. Maybe,
it came to me, a woman can take pleasure of her own?
Seize the future between her legs? Forward, he said.

Woman's House
Yoo Kim-Miles

The loud bang and scrape upstairs left Jessica in a panic. There was no way this was just the falling of a heavy object. There was a scrape after it, like a foot accidentally sliding across the floor. Jessica, all prepared to watch *You* on Netflix for her one night of freedom from her husband and kids, scrambled to the front door, sliding on her flip flops. With one hand on the handle of the storm door, she croaked, "Is someone there?"

It was 8:30, and the sky was turning a deep purple like a bruise after the pain subsides. There was a slight breeze leaving her feeling a bit chilly in her loose camisole and house shorts which were her gym shorts back in her college days. They were much too short for public wear now, but her husband Kevin always complimented her in them.

She called Kevin, but it went straight to voicemail. Why would he remember to bring a phone charger to a camping trip? What if they were attacked by a group of violent bandits in the deep forest? But she figured men don't think that far ahead. Or maybe they just don't think about those things at all. Danger doesn't lurk around every corner for them.

"Omg I heard a noise in the house. I think someone's in my house," Jess texted her two girlfriends. "What should I do?"

"Get out of there."

"Do you have your keys?" replied the other.

"Get a neighbor."

"Don't go back in until you get someone to check it out with you. You never know, especially for us these days."

"Ok." I texted back with trembling hands. Who do I ask?

Jessica scanned the street for cars in driveways. Many families were on vacation in the middle of July, so her eyes landed on Bill's house. He was walking back in from taking out his trash. He was about her age, 34 give or take, and he divorced about 4 years ago. Jess never saw his ex-wife or kid visit his house, so she assumed it was a contentious separation.

Bill never really came out of his house except to walk to his car to go to work or mow the lawn. Whenever their eyes met, she gave a slight smile, but he just stared at her, oftentimes long after she pulled her eyes away from his gaze. What was he looking at? Was it her long tan legs or her bare oppressive-summer-heat-outfit shoulders?

Or maybe he's checking out the rose bush behind you, you conceited bitch, she second-guessed herself.

Jessica took a few steps towards Bill's house and stopped short. She shivered. Maybe it was the warm breeze. Maybe it was the thought of inviting this man into her home to check out a noise. For all she knew, he could be just as dangerous as whatever was lurking in her bathtub. Or closet. Or behind the door. Or under the bed. The possibilities were endless.

She saw Bill's curtain move just slightly enough to know he was looking at her, standing in the middle of the street, walking toward his house. She instantly turned and walked up the path to the Gillman's door. She only saw one car, John's car, in the driveway, but sometimes she saw his wife Betty leave for the evening with her friends. Maybe he's home with the kids. He's always with the kids. Jess often saw him at the pool and local grocery store, two perfect monsters in tow. They exchanged pleasantries and short conversations about how small kids are like thieves, stealing all their money, food, time, and sanity.

Surely he won't think I'm crazy. He'll help me.

John struck her as a genuine good guy. His occasional Facebook posts were mostly of Betty and the kids, and they always included some shout-out to his beautiful and wonderful wife to whom he owed his entire adult existence as a man. People always commented underneath that he was lucky to have her and vice versa. He was the kind of guy who would help an old lady carry her groceries to the car. The kind who would tell a friend that the girl at the bar was too drunk. The kind who was taught by a sage father never to stare too long.

She walked up to his door and knocked three times, softly. No one answered, so she just rang the bell. Immediately a small dog started yapping, alerting them of a danger at the front door.

John opened the door with a frown, "Hi. What's up?"

"H-hey. I, um, thought I heard someone in my house upstairs. I called Kevin, but he's out camping with the kids and his buddies. I feel kind of silly calling the police... Is there a way you could come over and check it out with me? I don't know..." She felt her cheeks get hot at the mention of being scared and calling the police. What kind of Karen-type woman calls the police these days?

It would have helped if John smiled, but he just looked at her. Braless in a loose camisole with one strap falling off her bare shoulder. She quickly pulled the string up and crossed her arms, but there was no hiding the fact that she was nearly naked.

John glanced down at her legs and quickly looked back up toward her house. "So... Betty's going to be home in an hour. I'm just not sure if I should go over there with y- I mean- just alone. Can you just take a walk or something, and I'll go over with Betty when she gets home?"

"Yeah sure. That's ok. I mean... you don't want to be..." Her voice trailed off as she lost the idea she was trying to express. "You're busy. It's probably nothing."

"Betty will be home soon. She can come over to check on you later." John made every attempt not to look at Jessica, not her body, not her face, not her eyes. Definitely not her legs or shoulders. As his eyes remained fixed on the house behind her, he ignored her trembling hands.

"I think I'm fine. It's... nothing." Jess smiled the same smile she remembered giving to Bill on those hot July days. She couldn't tell whether she should be embarrassed or if she was causing him to feel embarrassed. For a fleeting moment, Jess had the feeling that she was the intruder, creeping in on his comfortable space. Either way, she knew she had to walk away quickly to save herself- or him- from any more humiliation.

"Have a good night. Sorry to bother you."

"You too. Hey, be careful out there!" John called out as she power-walked away from his door, from his barking dog, and from his avoidance of her very presence.

As Jessica turned the corner, she caught a glimpse of her

neighbor, old-man Vic, they called him even though he was only about 62. He was out smoking a cigarette near his shed.

"Oh, you're home!" Jess cried out in relief. "I didn't see your car."

"It's in the shop, young lady," Vic said in what could only be described as a typical old-man voice.

Old-man Vic was clearly an old-time kind of man. Maybe that's why he got his name. Most of his conversations with Kevin were about how he could make his lawn greener or power wash the siding to make the house look better. He sometimes threw in some jokes about how the wife is out shopping for home decor, you know, how wives like to do. "Happy wife, happy life," he would say. He often glanced over at Jessica and laughed at his own jokes. He sometimes complimented Jess on her hair or dress, looking her up and down, but it wasn't the same kind of stare as Bill. He looked at her and saw Kevin's wife, shopper of home decor and pretty dresses.

"Where's Kevin?"

"He's camping. I couldn't reach him. Listen. I swear I heard a noise upstairs 5 minutes ago. I think there might be someone in the house. I'm not sure. Can you just walk up with me to check?" Jess almost demanded. Surely, someone would want to help her. Some person must be willing to help her feel safe. In her own house.

"You heard a noise?" He repeated in a louder, even more old-man voice. "And you're scared?"

"Yes. It might be nothing, but I really feel like someone's up there."

Vic stubbed out his cigarette with his foot and started walking toward her door. Jessica followed. "I am going up there myself, and I will let you know if it is safe for you to go back in."

"But I just think it's safer for both-"

"Young lady. You are the smallest little thing I have seen. It would be safer for you out here. I will let you know." Vic climbed up her two steps and disappeared into the house.

Room by room, the light turned on and then off. Would he have checked under the beds? Would he have pulled the clothes to the side to check in the dark corners of the closets? Would he have opened up the shower door to look inside? Or did he just walk loudly, clunking his giant boots in an effort to scare off some intruder she had conjured up in her imagination?

Vic appeared back at the front door, a wide grin spread across his face. "I caught a 7-foot intruder hiding in your closet!"

Jess stared at him holding her breath in terror. She knew he was joking, but she wasn't laughing. The fear was real to her, apparently only to her.

"There's nothing up there, young lady," he bellowed as he continued shaking his head.

"Oh, thank you. Sorry. I guess..." Jessica stared at the windows on the second level. She was almost positive that there was someone up there. She could feel it.

The purple sky deepened into a dark gray, and all the street lights came on. The lights were supposed to make the residents feel safer, though all it did was make it possible to identify which neighbors were walking their dogs. Melanie from the next block walked by briskly. She was an athletic middle-aged woman who seemed to own all the matching yoga pants and tops from probably Kohl's or maybe Macy's on a fancy day. Jess wondered if John would have helped search her house for the 7-foot intruder. Or if her bare forearms and wrists were something to avoid as well.

"How ya doin'?" Melanie chirped.

Before Jess could end the conversation with a simple thumbs up, Vic chimed in, "Young lady here thought there was an intruder in her house. I just checked it out. Nothing to see."

"An intruder? Why?" Melanie's question indicated that she wanted details.

"I definitely heard-"

"She thought she heard a sound upstairs and wanted me to make sure there wasn't a criminal up there. I hate seeing young women scared like this, so I told her that I would go see alone."

Is he serious or is he mocking me?

"Well, I remember I thought someone was in my house years ago, but it was just my imagination. I think it was a shampoo bottle that fell off the ledge or something. I felt so silly calling my husband at work," Melanie added. "Sometimes we just think the world is more dangerous than it really is. Maybe we like the excitement or something."

We?

"I heard a scrape after a loud bang, like a foot sliding-"

"Oh, the shampoo bottle probably rolled after it fell!" Detective Melanie concluded. "Kevin's away on his camping trip with the kids, right? You must've been drinking wine. I know I would've jumped into that wine bottle, for sure!"

Melanie bobbed her head up and down emphatically as she spoke, seemingly in an attempt to assure Jess- or perhaps herself- that there was no real danger. She spoke with the confidence of an older, more experienced woman. Jessica wondered if Melanie remembered the fear of mysterious noises and shadowy corners. How long did it take to convince her that it was just a shampoo bottle? Just her emotions. Just her wild imagination. Jess wondered if Melanie still secretly checked on her shampoo bottle when she was home alone.

"No, it was a different noise. It was-"

"Well, listen, young lady. Let me give you my phone number in case you spook yourself again. You can call anytime, and I'll come over and set your mind at ease. I wouldn't want you getting scared and all worked up..."

Jessica tuned out her knight in shining armor. The one who chased away the big bad intruder with a pair of big bad boots. Had it all been in her imagination? Was she the hysterical woman people laughed at in viral videos? Had her giant shampoo bottle fallen off the ledge and rolled across the tub?

Somehow during the conversation, the detective dog walker had bid farewell and was already down to the next block. Vic secured his number into her phone and handed it back.

"You call me any time, and I will come over. Don't be scared." Vic winked and waited.

Jessica almost forgot her manners. "Thanks, Vic. You're my real-life hero."

She crept back into her house. Vic had left some of the lights on, so everything was bright. For minutes, she just stood by the front door, refusing to move into the intruder's trap. Despite Vic's reassurance, something told her that if there was a real danger, she would have to face it herself.

Eventually, she sat down on the closest chair to the front door in complete silence, jumping at every slight noise. The ice maker. A car driving down the street. A vibrating phone.

"What's up? Are you ok? What happened?" Her friend's text message inquired.

What had happened? She wondered.

"If you don't answer in a minute, I'm going to call the police to your house."

The threat of police lights on top of the embarrassment of recent events made Jessica immediately begin typing.

"I swear someone was in my house. I know-"

She erased it.

Or maybe something just fell, she second-guessed again. Despite the loud alarms sounded by her deepest conscience, she knew it would make more sense, be easier perhaps, to think it was the shampoo bottle. Maybe he is just staring at the rose bush. Maybe good guys don't see trembling hands. Maybe clunky boots could chase away a woman's fears. Maybe- maybe the shampoo bottle fell with a thud and rolled across the bathtub.

She reluctantly wrote back, "It was nothing. The neighbor checked. I was just overreacting. Probably a shampoo bottle falling or something."

Jessica braved herself to climb the steps to her bathroom. She tried to ignore the pounding of her heart, the surging of blood rushing to her head, the twitching of her eyelids, the trembling of her hands. With each step, her feet tingled beneath her. She whispered inaudible words as she tried to slow her rapid breathing.

Rose bush.

Hands.

Boots.

Shampoo bottle.

She inched closer to the master bedroom, ready to confront

her worst fear. Ready to laugh at her own hysterics. Ready to join Detective Melanie underneath the street lamps. She swung the shower door open. Sitting securely on the shower ledge was the purple shampoo bottle, fixed in its upright position.

Bios

Yoo Kim-Miles is a Maryland resident and a high school English teacher of 15 years. Spending years encouraging young people to develop their writing has inspired her to create her own work. Her first story, "Woman's House," explores a woman's perspective as she anticipates an outcome to her dilemma.

Pam McFarland is a Silver Spring, Md.-based writer and editor. She has an MA in fiction writing and has had work published or forthcoming by *Cobalt Review*, *The Saturday Evening Post*, and in an anthology of poems and stories by D.C. -area writers. She's working on her first novel.

Ricardo Gonzalez-Rothi - An academic physician and scientific writer, Ricardo has had his fiction, creative non-fiction and poetry featured in the U.S. and in the U.K., in Acentos Review, Hispanic Culture Review, Biostories, Foliate Oak,Lunch Ticket, The Bellingham Review, Molotov Cocktail, Star 82 Review, Wingless Dreamer, Litro and others. Born and raised in Cuba, he came to the United States as a refugee in his teens and now resides in North Florida. gonzalezrothiauthor.com

William Torphy's short stories have been featured in podcasts and have appeared in numerous magazines and journals, including Bryant Literary Review, The Fictional Café, Sun Star Quarterly, Chelsea Station, Arlington Literary Journal, and Adelaide Literary Magazine. His opinion pieces and reviews have been featured in Solstice Literary, OpEdge, Vox Populi and The Dalhousie Review. His short story collection, Motel Stories, was released by Unsolicited Press in March. He recently moved to Wisconsin from the San Francisco Bay Area where he served the arts community as an exhibition curator. www.williamtorphy.com

Rachel Kim Raczka is a writer based in Boston finishing her MFA in Creative Writing at Lesley University in Cambridge. She currently edits for The Boston Globe and teaches for Emerson College's Writing, Literature, and Publishing department and Brandeis University's Journalism Program. Her work has been published in the Washington Post, New York Magazine, Cherry Bombe, and Medium. She is working on her first young adult novel.

Susan Phillips Author of, "DEEP AUGUST," and "THE HEALING GROUND,"

James William Gardner writes extensively about the contemporary southland. The writer explores aspects of southern culture often overlooked: the downtrodden, the impoverished and those marginalized by society. His work has been nominated for the Pushcart Prize and Best of the Net. Gardner is a graduate of Virginia Commonwealth University and lives in Roanoke, Virginia. His work has appeared in numerous publications including Deep South Magazine, Newfound Journal and The Virginia Literary Journal.

Richard A. Ballou is a former executive with a multinational IT-consulting firm who retired from the business and technology arenas in his mid-forties to write literary fiction.His stories have been finalists or top-three finishers in numerous international contests,including the Calvino Prize, the Omnidawn Fabulist Fiction Chapbook Contest, the DorisBetts Fiction Competition, the Press 53 Open Awards, the Opossum Prize, and most recently, the annual contest sponsored by the Vincent Brothers Review. His writing goal is to engage and entertain while challenging and stretching the reader's field of vision.

Eva M. Schlesinger, *Literal Latte* Food Verse Award recipient and three-time Moth StorySLAM winner, is the author of four poetry chapbooks, including *Remembering the Walker & Wheelchair* and *Ode 2 Codes & Codfish*. Her work has appeared in Chicken Soup anthologies, the *San Francisco Chronicle, Readersdigest.com, Cerasus* Magazine, *Parentheses* Journal, and elsewhere. Eva is working on a short story collection and YA novel (that is, when she's not overwatering her plants).

Marah Reinoso Vega resides in Miami, Florida. She writes poetry, short fiction, and creative non-fiction about travel, education, and women's empowerment. Her work has appeared in The Hong Kong Review, Bright Flash Literary Review, The Bookends Review, and The Avalon Literary Review.

Dana Miller is a wicked wordsmith, giggling provocateuse, and mega-melomaniac from Atlanta, Georgia. Her poetic syllables like to trundle in the wilds—usually in search of a smackerel or two. On their way, they have found themselves featured in *Postscript Magazine, Better Than Starbucks, Fairy Piece, Sledgehammer Lit, FERAL: A Journal of Poetry and Art, Small Leaf Press, Tofu Ink Arts Press*, and *Nauseated Drive*. When not wielding a lethal pen, Dana adores surf culture, Australian grunge rockers, muscle cars, Epiphone guitars, glitter, Doc Martens, and medieval-looking draft horses with feathered feet. Oxford, England is her spirit-home and Radiohead is holding the last shard of her girlhood heart.

Linda Marshall -

Erika B. Girard is currently pursuing her M.A. in English and Creative Writing with a concentration in Poetry through SNHU. Originally from Rhode Island, she derives creative inspiration from her family, friends, faith, and fascination with the human experience. She is a proofreader for Wild Roof Journal, an online literary journal with issues published bimonthly. Her own creative work appears or is forthcoming in Black Fox, Iris Literary Journal, Untenured, Viewless Wings, and more.

Marisa P. Clark is a queer writer who grew up on the Mississippi Gulf Coast and came out in Atlanta. Her prose and poetry appear in Shenandoah, Cream City Review, Nimrod, Epiphany, Foglifter, Prairie Fire, Rust + Moth, Sundog Lit, Air/Light, and elsewhere. Best American Essays 2011 recognized her creative nonfiction among its Notable Essays. A senior fiction reader for New England Review, she lives in New Mexico with three parrots, two dogs, and whatever wildlife and strays stop to visit.

Chinua Ezenwa-Ohaeto -

Patrick Cabello Hansel is the author of the poetry collections The Devouring Land (Main Street Rag Publishing) and Quitting Time (Atmosphere Press) and the forthcoming Breathing in Minneapolis (Finishing Line Press). He has published poems and prose in over 85 journals, including Crannog, Ilanot Review, Hawai'i Pacific Review, Ash & Bones, RiverSedge and Lunch Ticket. Nominated three times for a Pushcart Prize, he has won awards from the Loft Literary Center and MN State Arts Board. His novella Searching was serialized in 33 issues of The Alley News. He is the editor of The Phoenix of Phillips, a literary journal by and for the most diverse community in Minneapolis. His website is: www.artecabellohansel.com

Gaylord Brewer is a professor at Middle Tennessee State University, where he founded and for 20+ years edited the journal Poems & Plays. The most recent of his 16 books of poetry, fiction, criticism, and cookery are two collections of poems, The Feral Condition (Negative Capability, 2018) and Worship the Pig (Red Hen, 2020). A book of flash nonfiction, Before the Storm Takes It Away, is forthcoming from Red Hen in spring 2024.

Sarath Reddy -

Terri Drake is a graduate of the Iowa Writers' Workshop. Her poetry collection, "At the Seams" was published by Bear Star Press. Her chapbook, "Regarding Us," was recently published by Finishing Line Press. Her poems have appeared in The Chicago Quarterly Review; Crab Creek Review; Poets Reading the News; Heavy Feather Review; Quarry West, Perihelion; Heartwood

Literary Magazine; and Open: Journal of Art and Letters, among others. She is a practicing psychoanalyst living in Santa Cruz, California.

Charlotte Friedman is a poet, translator and teacher who grew up in the Pacific Northwest and now lives in New Jersey. Her nonfiction book, The Girl Pages, was published by Hyperion, and her poetry in journals such as Connecticut River Review, Intima and Waterwheel Review. Her translations of Ch'ol poetry (with Carol Rose Little) have been published in World Literature Today, The Arkansas International and elsewhere. She taught narrative medicine at Barnard College for ten years, as well as in hospitals in New York and Israel.

Kurt Olsson has published two poetry collections. His second, *Burning Down Disneyland*(Gunpowder Press), won the Barry Spacks Prize. Olsson's first collection, *What Kills What Kills Us* (Silverfish Review Press), won the Gerald Cable Book Award and was subsequently awarded the Towson University Prize for Literature, given to the best book published the previous year by a Maryland writer. A third collection, *The Unnumbered Anniversaries,* is due out later this year or early next. Olsson's poems have appeared in many journals, including *Poetry, The New Republic, Southern Review,* and *The Threepenny Review.*

Rohan Buettel lives in Canberra, Australia. His haiku have appeared in various Australian and international journals (including Frogpond, Cattails and The Heron's Nest). His longer poetry recently appears in The Goodlife Review, Rappahannock Review, Penumbra Literary and Art Journal, Mortal Magazine, Passengers Journal, Reed Magazine, Meniscus and Quadrant.

Frankie A Soto is a 2x winner of the Multicultural Poet of the year award from the National Spoken Word Poetry Awards in Chicago. His (New York Times) performance called him an absolute force. He's been featured on ABC news, FOX & his HIV poem "Guessing Game" was nominated & premiered at the

Atlanta Hip Hop Festival. His poem "Spanglish" is widely used as part of the curriculum at Colleges/ Universities around the country & partnered with HBO for Hispanic heritage month promo. His current manuscript 'Petrichor' was a semi-finalist for the 2021 Hudson Prize with Black Lawrence Press & was a top three finalist for the 2021 Sexton Prize with Black Spring Press in London & is now being published with Tolsun Books in 2024.

Torrey Francis Malek is a poet hailing from northern Delaware. Torrey expresses his passion through poetry, prose, and short-story fiction while covering a wide variety of subjects, centered usually on observation, family dynamics, history, and mental health, often from a humorist's perspective.

Mary Beth O'Connor recently retired from twenty years of teaching in Ithaca, New York. She is a writer, watercolor painter, and grandma. Her poetry and prose have appeared in The Healing Muse, Minerva Rising, Passager, Sliver of Stone, Blast Furnace, Painted Bride Quarterly, Blueline, Café Irreal, Prick of the Spindle, and other literary magazines. Her chapbook Smackdown! Poems about the Professor Business was the winner of the first Teachers' Voice poetry chapbook competition.

Jennifer Fossenbell's poetry, prose, and linguistic experiments have appeared in Black Warrior Review, Alluvium, The Volta, So & So, Posit, and other publications, as well as in literary festivals and multigenre exhibitions in the U.S., China, and Vietnam. She co-translates Chinese poetry for Spittoon Literary Journal, and has also edited translations of Vietnamese poetry for two collections plus numerous exhibitions and a radio show. She completed her MFA at the University of Minnesota and now lives in the northern suburbs of Denver, USA, where she works as a web crafter, cat mom, human mom, and tender of two grandmother pines. More at jenniferfossenbell.com.

Arshia Batra is a writer and photographer in Seattle, Washington. Her poetry has appeared in October Hill Magazine and Last Leaves Magazine, and she is a Pushcart Prize nominee. She attends the University of Washington, working towards a psychology degree.

A New Englander with long farming roots, **Karen Kilcup** is the Elizabeth Rosenthal Excellence Professor of American Literature, Environmental & Sustainability Studies, and Women's, Gender, & Sexuality Studies at UNC Greensboro. Her forthcoming poetry collection The Art of Restoration was awarded the 2021 Winter Goose Poetry Prize, and her forthcoming chapbook Red Appetite received the 2022 Helen Kay Chapbook Poetry Prize. She's an avid cook, runner, kayaker, and rock climber who has difficulty resisting the urge for More Garden.

Elizabeth Taryn Mason once worked at an amusement park, but now she is an Associate Professor at Mount St. Joseph University in Cincinnati, OH where she teaches composition, literature and creative writing and serves as faculty advisor for the student-operated literary magazine. When she's not grading papers or in her office, you can usually find her with a pen in her hand, her nose in a book, or cheering at a baseball game with her husband and her little boy.

Theadora Siranian's poetry has appeared in Best New Poets, Ghost City Press, and Atticus Review, among others. In 2014, she was shortlisted for the Mississippi Review Prize and Southword's Gregory O'Donoghue International Poetry Prize. In 2019, Theadora received the Emerging Woman Poet Honor from Small Orange Journal. Her chapbook, She, was released by Seven Kitchens Press in May 2021. More of her work can be found at theadorasiranian.com.

Jana Harris teaches creative writing at the University of Washington and at the Writer's Workshop in Seattle. She is editor and founder of Switched-on Gutenberg. Her most recent publications are You Haven't Asked About My Wedding or What I

Wore; Poems of Courtship on the American Frontier (University of Alaska Press) and the memoir, Horses Never Lie About Love (Simon & Schuster). She lives with her husband on a farm in the Cascades.

After a newspaper career, **Eric Chiles** began teaching writing and journalism at colleges in eastern Pennsylvania. He is the author of the chapbook "Caught in Between," and his poetry has appeared in The American Journal of Poetry, Canary, Chiron Review, Gravel, Main Street Rag, Plainsongs, Rattle, Tar River Poetry, and elsewhere. In 2014 he completed a 10-year section hike of the Appalachian Trail.

Shaun Anthony McMichael - Since 2007, Shaun has taught writing to students from around the world, in classrooms, juvenile detention halls, mental health treatment centers, and homeless youth drop-ins throughout the Seattle area. Over 70 of his works have appeared in literary magazines, online, and in print. He lives in Seattle with his wife and son. Visit him at his website shaunanthonymcmichael.com.

Valerie Wong (AKA @theglutenfreepoet on Instagram) was born in Toronto, raised in Hong Kong and is currently a management consultant in New York. As a Third Culture Kid, she is a local and a foreigner wherever she goes. Valerie's poetry has been published by journals around the world, including Stanford University's Mantis, the League of Canadian Poets' Poetry Pause and New Zealand's Blackmail Press. Her writing has been used as discussion material at Yokohama International School, and will be featured in RiskPress's Processing Crisis, a multi-genre anthology to be published in spring 2022. She is currently editing her first novel.

Elise Chadwick taught English at Horace Greeley High School in Chappaqua, NY for 30 years. She lives in NYC and upstate NY. Her poems have been recently published in *The Paterson Literary Review*, *Healing Muse*, *Literary Mama* and *The English*

Journal.

Alice B Fogel was the New Hampshire poet laureate (2015-2019). Her latest collection of 6 is Nothing But, a series of poems responding to Abstract Expressionism and its effect on our consciousness. Others are A Doubtful House and Interval: Poems Based on Bach's "Goldberg Variations," which won the Nicholas Schaffner Award for Music in Literature and the 2016 NH Literary Award in Poetry. Recipient of an NEA fellowship, she works one-on-one with neurodiverse students at Landmark College.

Kristin Camitta Zimet is the author of a full-length collection of poems, Take in My Arms the Dark, and the editor of The Sow's Ear Poetry Review. Her poetry is published in journals and anthologies around the world and has been performed in venues from concert halls to arboretums. She is also a visual artist, a Virginia Master Naturalist, and a Reiki healer.

Naomi Bess Leimsider has published poems, flash fiction, and short stories in Packingtown Review, Tangled Locks Journal, The Avenue Journal, Booth, Anti-Heroin Chic, Wild Roof Journal, Planisphere Quarterly, Little Somethings Press, Syncopation Literary Journal, On the Seawall, St. Katherine Review, Exquisite Pandemic, Orca, Hamilton Stone Review, Rogue Agent Journal, Coffin Bell Journal, Hole in the Head Review, Newtown Literary, Otis Nebula, Quarterly West, The Adirondack Review, Summerset Review, Blood Lotus Journal, Pindeldyboz, 13 Warriors, Slow Trains, Zone 3, Drunkenboat, and The Brooklyn Review. She has been a finalist for the Acacia Fiction Prize, the Saguaro Poetry Prize, and the Tiny Fork Chapbook Contest. Also, she received a Pushcart Prize nomination for fiction in 2022. In addition, her poetry chapbook, *Wild Evolution*, will be published by Cathexis Northwest Press in Fall 2023.

Alice Friman's seventh collection is Blood Weather, LSU Press, 2019. Her last two, also from LSU, are The View from Saturn and Vinculum, which won the Georgia author of the year award in poetry. A recipient of two Pushcart Prizes and included in Best American Poetry, she's won many prizes and has been been published in Poetry, Ploughshares, Plume, Georgia Review, Gettysburg Review, Crazyhorse, Poetry East, Massachusetts Review, and many others. Her website is alicefrimanpoet.com.

Jo Angela Edwins has published poems in various venues including recently or forthcoming in The Hollins Critic, The Hyacinth Review, Mom Egg Review, and Rabid Oak. Her chapbook Play was published in 2016 by Finishing Line Press, and her full-length collection A Dangerous Heaven is forthcoming this year from Gnashing Teeth Publishing. She lives in Florence, SC, where she teaches at Francis Marion University and serves as poet laureate of the Pee Dee region of South Carolina.

J.R. Solonche is the author of 29 books of poetry and coauthor of another. He has been nominated for the National Book Award and twice nominated for the Pulitzer Prize. He lives in the Hudson Valley.

Sekani Johnson is an emerging poet and photographer from Detroit, Michigan who decided to stop hoarding his talent.

Louise Wilford lives and works in Yorkshire, UK. She's been writing poetry and prose since childhood. Her work has been widely published, most recently in *805, Last Leaves, New Verse News, Pine Cone Review, Punk Noir, River and South, Silver Blade, The Avenue, POTB, Balloons Lit, Parakeet, The Fieldstone Review*, and *Black Hare Press*. In 2020, she won the £750 First Prize in the Arts Quarterly Short Story Competition, and was awarded a Masters in Creative Writing (Distinction) from the Open University. She is working on a fantasy novel. You can read her blog here: https://louviewsnewscues. blogspot.com/